E<small>NJOY A</small> [...]
T<small>HE</small> G<small>UARDI</small> [...]

Book One: *The Capture*

Book Two: *The Journey*

Book Three: *The Rescue*

Book Four: *The Siege*

Book Five: *The Shattering*

Book Six: *The Burning*

Book Seven: *The Hatchling*

Book Eight: *The Outcast*

Book Nine: *The First Collier*

Book Ten: *The Coming of Hoole*

Book Eleven: *To Be a King*

Book Twelve: *The Golden Tree*

Beyond the Beyond

Shadow Forest

Silverveil

Southern
Kingdoms

The Barrens

Forest
Kingdom
of
Ambala

St. Aegolius Canyons

N

St. Aegolius Academy
for Orphaned Owls

Broken Talon Point

Northern Kingdoms

Peninsula of the Spirit Woods

Ice Narrows

Sea of Hoolemere

Island of Hoole

Cape Glaux

The Beaks

Desert of Kuneer

Forest Kingdom of Tyto

Soren's Hollow

River Hoole

As Dewlap lashed out in futile desperation against the wind and water,
the book she had left on the rock tumbled end over end into the sea.

GUARDIANS
of GA'HOOLE

BOOK FOUR
The Siege

BY KATHRYN LASKY

SCHOLASTIC INC.

New York Toronto London Auckland Sydney
Mexico City New Delhi Hong Kong Buenos Aires

No part of this publication may be reproduced in whole or in part, or stored in a retrieval system, or transmitted in any form or by any means, electronic, mechanical, photocopying, recording, or otherwise, without written permission of the publisher. For information regarding permission, write to Scholastic Inc., Attention: Permissions Department, 557 Broadway, New York, NY 10012.

ISBN 0-439-40560-2

Artwork by Richard Cowdrey
Design by Steve Scott

12 11 10   6 7 8 9/0

Printed in the U.S.A.   40

First printing, May 2004

Northern Kingdoms

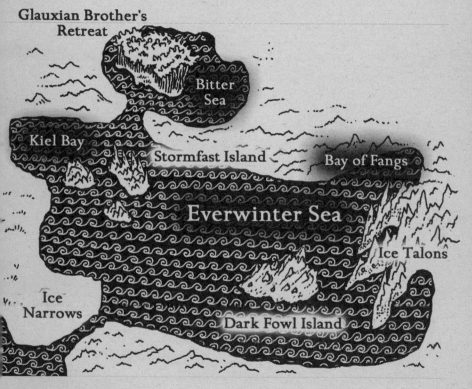

Glauxian Brother's
Retreat

Bitter
Sea

Kiel Bay

Stormfast Island

Bay of Fangs

Everwinter Sea

Ice Talons

Ice
Narrows

Dark Fowl Island

Southern
Kingdoms

Contents

Author's Note

Winston Churchill was Prime Minister of England during World War II. For months, citizens of London were subjected to ceaseless bombings by the Nazis. It was called the Battle of Britain and the courage of the men, women, and children was remarkable during this terrifying time. Churchill's radio addresses helped rally an exhausted and frightened nation. It was said that Winston Churchill was the man who mobilized the English language. I would like to acknowledge a great debt to Churchill, for I very closely modeled many of Ezylryb's speeches in Chapters Eighteen, Twenty, and Twenty-two after some of Mr. Churchill's most stirring addresses.

When I was a child, a popular reply to a bully was: "Sticks and stones will break my bones, but words will never hurt me."

Now that I am an adult, I think this is not true. Words can hurt. But I never would have dreamed back then when I was a child that words like Mr. Churchill's could give such courage, strength, stamina, and valor to the citizens who were facing the most horrific circumstances of war.

Prologue

Sparks flew off his beak as the owl, mad with rage, careened through the night sky. "I must find water! I must find water! This mask will melt my eyes. Glaux blood on my brother's gizzard!" The Barn Owl screeched as his glowing beak sliced the blackness of the night. The curse, the worst that an owl could say, seemed to relieve Kludd of the terrible feelings that stormed within him. But hate still fed him, fed his flight, fed his desperate search for a cool pond in which to plunge his mask of molten metal, his singed feathers set aflame by his brother, Soren, in a battle that had gone wrong. All wrong!

Below, he spotted the glint of the moon off a smooth liquid surface. Water! The huge Barn Owl banked and began to spiral downward. Soon, cool water. He had lost his beak in one battle. He had lost all of his face feathers in another. His ear slits had been scarred this time but he still had one eye and, most important, he still had his hatred. Kludd fed and coddled his hatred as a mother owl fed and coddled her baby chicks.

Thank Glaux he still could hate!

CHAPTER ONE
The Pilgrim

The Brown Fish Owl looked up and blinked. The red comet had passed by for the last time nearly three months before. What could this glowing point in the sky be? It was hurtling toward the lake at an alarming speed. Great Glaux, it was screeching the most horrid, foulest oaths imaginable!

The Brown Fish Owl stepped farther out on the sycamore branch that extended over the lake. If this were not a Fish Owl, it would need rescuing. Most species of owls, save for Fish Owls and Eagle Owls, were completely helpless in the water. The Brown Fish Owl began to spread his wings and was ready to flap them quickly for a power take-off. Within the sliver of a second before he heard the splash, he was off.

There was a sizzling sound as Kludd hit the water, and then there were wisps of steam. Simon, the Brown Fish Owl, had never seen anything like this — an owl glowing like a coal from a forest fire, plunging into the pond. Was it a collier owl? But colliers would know better. Remarkable as it seemed, a collier owl could do its work without ever getting burned. The Brown Fish Owl grabbed the mysterious owl with his talons just in time. But his gizzard went cold as he saw the owl's face — a mangled deformity of molten metal and feathers. What was this?

Well, better not worry now. At least it was alive, and as a pilgrim owl of the Glauxian Brothers of the Northern Kingdoms, Simon's duty was not to question, nor convert, nor preach, but simply to help, give solace, peace, and love. This owl seemed sorely in need of all. And this was precisely why the brothers took seasons away from their retreat and study; to go out into the world and fulfill their sacred obligation. The Brother Superior often said, "To study too much in retreat can become an inexcusable indulgence. It behooves us to share what we have learned, to practice in administering to others what we have gathered from our experience with books."

This was Pilgrim Simon's first season of pilgrimming and this seemed to be his first big challenge. The burned owl would need tending. No doubt about it. Restoring fallen owlets to nests, making peace between warring factions of crows — the Glauxian Brothers were among the few owls who could speak sense to crows — all that was nothing compared to this. It would take all of Simon's medicinal and herbal knowledge to fix up this poor owl.

"Easy there, easy there, fellow," Simon spoke in a low soothing voice as he helped the wounded owl into the hollow of the sycamore. "We're going to fix you up just fine." This was when Simon could have used a nest-maid snake or two. What a luxury they had been back at the retreat in the Northern Kingdoms. But here the pilgrims were charged to live simply. To avail themselves of the blind snakes that tended so many owls' nests, keeping them free of vermin, was not deemed appropriate for the pilgrim owls who were dedicated to service. They had been instructed to live as sparely as possible. Simon would have to go out and dig the medicinal worms himself. Leeches were the best for healing these kinds of wounds, and being a Fish Owl, he was fairly adept at leech gathering.

As soon as Simon had Kludd arranged in the hollow on a soft bed made of down plucked from his own breast and a combination of mosses, he set out to gather the leeches. As he flew to a corner of the lake that was rich with leeches, he reflected on how this owl, which might be a Barn Owl, had fought when he had tried to preen him. This was very odd. He had never known an owl who had resisted being preened. This owl's feathers were a dirty, tangled mess. That he could have flown at all was amazing. Smooth flight depended on smooth feathers. On every flight feather there were tiny almost invisible hooks, or barbules, that locked together to produce an even surface over which the air could glide. This owl's barbules had become unhooked in the worst way. They needed to be lined up and smoothed out again. But when Simon had first tried, the owl had pulled away. Odd, very odd.

Simon returned in a short while with a beakful of leeches and began placing them around the curled edges of the strange metal mask that had melted over most of the owl's face. He didn't dare try to remove it. Upon closer examination, Simon was sure that this was a Barn Owl, an exceptionally large one at that. With patches of soaked moss, he squeezed drops of water into the owl's beak. Occasionally, the owl's eyes would flutter open, but he was clearly delirious. In this state he spewed a nearly constant stream of curses laced with tirades of vengeance and death addressed to some creature he called Soren.

Day and night Simon treated the strange Barn Owl, changing the leeches, squeezing drops of water beneath the twisted piece of metal that was where a beak must once have been. The owl's agitation calmed; the rancorous curses fewer — most thankfully, for the Brothers of Glaux were a gentle order who eschewed fighting. For two days the Barn Owl had slept long uninterrupted stretches, and now on the third day, his eyes blinked open. Simon could tell that he was fully conscious at last. But the first words out of that metallic beak shocked the pilgrim Brown Fish Owl almost as much as the curses had. "You are not a Pure One."

A Pure One? What in the name of Glaux is this owl talking about? "Forgive me, but I am afraid I do not understand what you are talking about," said Simon.

Kludd blinked. *He should be afraid.* "Never mind. I suppose I must thank you."

"Oh, don't suppose anything. You need not thank me. I am a pilgrim. I am merely doing my Glauxian duty."

"Duty to what?"

"Duty to our species."

"You are not of my species!" Kludd barked with a ferocity that shocked the Fish Owl. "I am a Barn Owl, *Tyto alba*. You are" — Kludd seemed to sniff — "judging from your stink, a Fish Owl — not my species."

"Well, I was speaking generally, of course. My Glauxian duty extends to all owlkind."

Kludd responded with a low, growlish hoot and shut his eyes.

"I'll leave you now," said Simon.

"If you're going hunting, I would prefer red meat to fish — vole, to be precise."

"Yes, yes. I'll do my best. I'm sure you'll be feeling better as soon as I get you some meat."

Kludd glared at the Brown Fish Owl. *You can be sure of nothing with me. Glaux, what an ugly owl — flattish head, muddled color, not quite brown, not quite gray or white. Miserable little ear tufts. It doesn't get much uglier than a Brown Fish Owl, that's for sure.*

Kludd, however, thought he had heard of these pilgrim-type owls. Might as well learn a bit more. "So you say you're a pilgrim. Where are you from?"

Simon was delighted that the Barn Owl was taking any notice at all. "The Northern Kingdoms."

This interested Kludd. He had heard of the Northern Kingdoms. That was where the ancient and brilliant owl Ezylryb, whom he had almost captured, had come from. It was because of Ezylryb that he had nearly died in this last battle. "I thought the Northern Kingdoms were known for their warriors, not pilgrims."

"Owls of the Northern Kingdoms are very fierce, but one can be fierce in love and in peace as well as in hatred and in battle."

Glaux, this owl frinked him off. Made him want to

yarp a dozen pellets right in his ugly face. "I see," Kludd said. But of course he didn't see at all. Still, sometimes diplomacy was necessary. And this was what Kludd considered a diplomatic response to an owl that made his gizzard turn green.

"Well, why don't you fly off and get me some good red meat, nice and furry, good bones — my gizzard needs something to grind." *And I need time to think.*

The Northern Kingdoms! The mere mention of them by the disgusting Brown Fish Owl had set Kludd's mind ablaze. He had to plan carefully now. The capture of the old Whiskered Screech Ezylryb had failed miserably. Of course, one hardly could have called it a great scheme. No, the great scheme had been to build a force large enough to lay siege to St. Aegolius Academy for Orphaned Owls, better known as St. Aggie's. The academy had been snatching owlets for years and training them to mine flecks, among other things. With flecks, one could create weapons of unbelievable power. Not simply weapons that killed, but weapons that could warp the minds of owls. St. Aggie's had the largest known supply of flecks. But the owls of St. Aggie's didn't know what to do with them. Still, ignorant as they were, they had found the stronghold of the Pure Ones in the castle ruins and tried to make off with the owlets that Kludd and scores of Tytos had captured. The Pure Ones, of course, fought back to recover what was, in their minds, rightfully theirs. This resulted in the Great Downing. Scores of baby owls dropped while the two powerful and lawless forces battled it out. And it was the Great Downing that had alerted the owl world — in particular, those noble owls, known as the Guardians of Ga'Hoole, who rose in the darkness of the night from the Great Ga'Hoole Tree — that there was something out there more fearful than St. Aggie's.

Before the Great Downing, the organization of the Pure Ones had been secret, and this state afforded them valuable time and opportunity to build their forces and develop their strategies. The Great Downing had brought the Ga'Hoolian owls out in full force. And, most significantly, it had brought out the legendary warrior from the Northern Kingdoms, known there as Lyze of Kiel and now in the Southern Kingdoms as Ezylryb. But it was not Lyze of Kiel the warrior who had interested Kludd. It was Ezylryb the scholar. It was said that this owl had the deepest knowledge of everything — from weather, to fire, to the very elements of life and the earth. And this owl best understood the lurking powers of the flecks.

So when the Pure Ones had lost the owlets, their source for new owl power, Kludd had abruptly decided to change tactics. The capture of one owl like Ezylryb would be worth more than one hundred baby owls. The only way he could think of capturing the old one was through a Devil's Triangle. By placing three bags of flecks in three different trees to form a triangle, Kludd had laid a trap that had ensnared the old Whiskered Screech by causing massive disruptions to his powers of navigation. The flecks set up a magnetic field. That this field had been broken was not only unexpected, but disastrous. And it had been broken. Other owls had come to Ezylryb's rescue. They had snapped the power of this field as if it had been no more than a brittle twig. Higher magnetics! Ezylryb knew these dark sciences. And that was why Kludd had wanted him.

There had been a fierce battle with the owls who had come to rescue Ezylryb. Much to Kludd's horror, one of them had been his own baby brother, Soren, whom he had pushed out of the family's nest when Soren was an owlet too young to fly. At the time, Kludd thought that he had been delivering up his younger brother to the Grand Tyto Most Pure, for that had been the requirement — to sacrifice a family member and thus assure one's own admission to the highest ranks of the Pure Ones. But something had gone wrong. St. Aggie's had shown up and taken his brother. Now this very brother had nearly killed him. And not only had the Pure Ones had their new recruits stolen from them, not only had they lost Ezylryb, but their stronghold had been discovered. They needed to find a new place to roost, a headquarters from which to plan their war for supremacy.

Well, no need to think about all that now. There were other more important matters — like higher magnetics. *All this time*, Kludd thought, *I have dreamed of flecks, of controlling the owl universe and making it pure. I have dreamed of conquering St. Aggie's, with its great reservoirs of flecks and its thousands of owls to mine them. And then I dreamed of capturing Ezylryb. But now I know what I must do. I must lay siege to the great tree on the Island of Hoole, in the middle of the Sea of Hoolemere. Yes, the Great Ga'Hoole Tree must be ours, with its secrets of fire and magnetics, with its warriors and its scholars, it must be ours. I shall bide my time. I shall gain my strength. I shall find my scattered army and then we shall rise — rise a thousand times more powerful than we ever were, against the Guardians of Ga'Hoole.*

"A nice plump vole for you, sir. Strong bones and plenty of fur. Its winter pelt is fully grown. That should set your gizzard grinding just fine." The Brown Fish Owl pilgrim had just returned.

Yes, and so will you, pilgrim. For Kludd had decided that upon regaining his strength, he would kill this owl immediately. His own survival must remain a secret for some time if all his plans were to work. Yes, by tomorrow with the vole's bones like grist in his gizzard, he would be ready to kill the stinking Brown Fish Owl. Kludd, like the best of killers, was patient.

CHAPTER TWO
The Watcher in the Woods

Some might have thought her a scroom, a ghost owl, but she was not. Her feathers had turned a misty gray color with spots of white. She was, indeed, a Spotted Owl, but an odd one. She had perched in a tree not far from the sycamore. Her wings, slightly crippled, made long flights difficult and, when she did fly, her path was often crooked. Nonetheless, she went out scouting every day.

She was almost invisible to the others in Ambala. When they saw her, which was seldom, they called her Mist. But although she was not often seen, she seemed to see all. When she sensed danger or saw something disturbing, she flew to the eagles with whom she shared a nest. In the past, there had been slipgizzles to keep an eye on such things. But since the Barred Owl who had watched in the borderlands between The Beaks and Ambala had been murdered, there had been no one. Now the owl called Mist sensed that there was great peril nearby.

She had watched the strange sight a few nights before

when a smoldering owl had plunged into the lake. She had seen the pilgrim owl rescue it and had been amazed when she observed the pilgrim flying out to fetch leeches. She could not imagine how that owl had survived its plunge, let alone the embers that encrusted its face. But it must have, for the next day, she had seen the good pilgrim go out hunting, and had heard him fretting over finding a vole. He was muttering to himself in a taut voice that the injured owl had demanded meat and not fish. Mist could not imagine how that owl could be so demanding of the pilgrim who had saved his life. And now she watched as the pilgrim went out several times each day and always for red meat — rat, vole, squirrel, but never fish.

She had become more and more curious about the owl recovering in the hollow of the sycamore. How close did she dare come? Most animals in this forest, especially owls, never really saw her. They looked through her. To them she appeared like fog or mist. But even when they did see her, they never seemed to recognize her as an owl, or as any creature they knew. And this was fine with her. The only ones who did know her were the eagles with whom she lived, Zan and Streak.

So she crept forward on the branch of the fir tree where she perched. It was a short flight to the spruce that grew next to the sycamore where the wounded owl was recovering. A few minutes later, she lighted down onto the spruce. There was one branch that extended farther than the others and nearly touched the sycamore. From this branch she had a perfect view into the hollow where the wounded owl rested. The Spotted Owl gasped at what she saw. The injured owl was immense and his face was hidden behind a metal mask that made him appear horrifyingly brutal. She felt her gizzard twitch and a slow dread begin to build. She must get back to the eagles. There was something about this owl that was more evil than anything she had ever seen. But just then, she heard the approach of the pilgrim. Suddenly, the entire world seemed to turn into a blizzard of bloody feathers. A terrible shriek shattered the forest. And then it was over. In a matter of seconds, the Brown Fish Owl lay dead on the forest floor. One wing ripped off, his head nearly split open. As the blackness of the night gathered in the forest, the huge owl with the metal mask raised its wings up, then flapped and lifted into the sky.

The Spotted Owl's gizzard turned to ice as the owl settled on the very same limb upon which she perched. She had survived so much. Was she now to die in the talons of this monster owl? The monster turned toward her. The Spotted Owl dared not breathe. Never had she perched this close to an owl and remained imperceptible. The monster blinked. *Incredible! He sees straight through me. I am indeed mist.*

The branch shook as Kludd flapped his wings again and rose into the night to seek his Pure Ones. With this murder finished, the time for revenge had arrived. Vengeance and glory would be his. His gizzard quivered in exultation. A silent scream filled his brain. *Kludd Rules Supreme!*

CHAPTER THREE
At the Great Ga'Hoole Tree

The big limbs of the Great Ga'Hoole Tree shook with the blasts from the first winter's gale. It was the season of the white rain, when the vines that hung from the tree turned a glistening ivory. The best of the milkberries had all been harvested weeks before in the time of the copper-rose rain, when the vines were burnished a deep copper-rose color. The weather chaw to which Soren belonged had just returned from an interpretation flight led by Ezylryb, captain of the chaw. It had been Ezylryb's first flight since his rescue from the Devil's Triangle. And it had been wonderful — a loud, boisterous mission with plenty of wet poop jokes and singing. But they had come back with good information despite Otulissa's dire prediction that they would learn nothing if they didn't stop all the gleeking about. Gleeking was the owl word for messing around and not being serious. Some chaw leaders such as Strix Struma never permitted such gleeking, but Ezylryb was different. He believed that gleeking was good, building trust and fellowship.

Otulissa, however, a serious and proper young Spotted Owl, abhorred gleeking about in general, and wet poop jokes in particular. It was a never-ending debate between her and Soren.

"Soren, I just don't believe that exchanging wet poop jokes with seagulls should be part of any mission."

Otulissa and Soren, both members of the weather chaw, perched on a branch just outside the dining hollow waiting for Matron to announce that breaklight was ready. Breaklight was the meal the owls enjoyed at the end of the night, just before the break of dawn. After this, they would sleep for the rest of the daylight hours until the evening shadows began to creep over the earth and darken the sky.

"You can learn a lot from seagulls, Otulissa," Soren was saying.

"I beg to differ. All that churring and guffawing and giggling over their pathetic humor interrupts the pressure-front vibrations." Spotted Owls were known for their extreme sensitivities to atmospheric pressure that came with changes in the weather.

"Well, you picked up on the fact that a blizzard was behind this gale, and look, it's starting to snow now. So I don't see how it damaged your prediction."

"Soren, I could have predicted a lot more precisely when and how much snow we would be getting if there hadn't been all that gleeking about. Also, I just don't find wet poop jokes funny. As owls, we should be proud of our digestive system and our unique manner of eliminating waste."

"Oh, it's *yarping*, for Glaux's sake." A large Great Gray Owl named Twilight had just lighted down onto the branch next to them. Twilight was one of Soren's closest friends.

"It's not simply yarping, Twilight. That we pack the bones and fur of our waste into neat little packets for excretion is quite extraordinary in the bird kingdom. That so little of our waste is liquid is exceptional. Yarping pellets through our mouths is magnificent," said Otulissa.

"Seen one pellet, seen them all," Twilight growled.

"I'm getting cold," Soren said. "When is breaklight going to be ready? I, for one, am ready for something hot."

Before a mission, the owls of the weather chaw were not permitted to eat their food cooked. Ezylryb insisted that they eat their food raw and with all the "hair" — as he called it — on the meat. Of course, the owls of the

Ga'Hoole Tree were special in that they often ate cooked food. Most owls ate their food raw and bloody because, unlike the owls of the great tree, they did not possess the extensive knowledge of fire. The owls of the Great Ga'Hoole Tree enjoyed a civilization unrivaled by any of the other kingdoms of owls. With their knowledge, they tried to protect the lives of owls in other kingdoms. Lately, however, the dangers had increased alarmingly. Not the least of these dangers were the evil owls of St. Aegolius Academy for Orphaned Owls where Soren had once been imprisoned. At St. Aggie's, he had met his best friend Gylfie, an Elf Owl. And now there was an even more destructive group, the Pure Ones. It had been on the mission to rescue Ezylryb that Soren had discovered that his own brother, Kludd, was the leader of this group.

Matron, a bunchy Barred Owl, poked her beak out of an opening near the branch where Soren and the others perched. "Breaklight!" she announced cheerfully.

"At last!" Soren said.

"Ooh, bats! I smell roasted bat wings!" Gylfie suddenly swooped in.

"Where've you been?" Soren turned to the Elf Owl.

"Helping Octavia in the library," she replied.

"Octavia in the library? Why?" Soren asked.

"Orders from the top, I guess. We were supposed to organize all the books on higher magnetics and flecks." Soren felt his gizzard lurch. He would never get used to hearing the word "flecks."

"But Octavia? Why Octavia? What use is a blind snake in the library? No offense, Mrs. P.," Otulissa asked as they crowded around Mrs. Plithiver, another blind snake.

"None taken, dear," the rosy-colored snake replied.

For centuries, blind snakes had served as maids in the nests of owls, keeping them free of vermin and pests. In the Great Ga'Hoole Tree, they served in other tasks as well. Among such tasks were providing the dining tables upon which the owls ate. They could easily and quickly extend their bodies to accommodate more diners.

Answering Otulissa's question, Gylfie replied, "Why Octavia? Well, she might be blind, but she has served Ezylryb for so long that she knows which books he wants on the special reserve shelf for higher magnetics. And it was too much work for just the book matron. She doesn't know the collection as well as Octavia — at least not these books. But then, of course, Dewlap came in and started bossing us around."

There was a sigh from the owls. Dewlap was the most boring teacher, or ryb, of the Great Ga'Hoole Tree.

"What's *she* doing in the library?" Soren asked. "Higher magnetics has nothing to do with the stuff she teaches."

Otulissa plumped up her feathers. "Oh, never mind. I am just so excited about studying higher magnetics, I can't tell you."

"Then don't," said Twilight.

"Yes, spare us, learned one," Gylfie said under her breath in a barely audible whisper to Soren, who laughed. Otulissa was a very smart owl. No one would deny that. She had been the one to figure out how the Devil's Triangle worked, and how to destroy it with fire. And she knew of the protective qualities of mu metal that guarded against the hazards of the magnetic flecks. But she wasn't shy about flaunting her knowledge, and sometimes it became boring. Especially now as she began talking about her long list of distinguished relatives who were all scholars, in particular the genius, long gone, great-great-great-aunt of hers, Strix Emerilla, who had written countless scientific books. It was always Strix Emerilla this or Strix Emerilla that. After a little while, the other owls at Mrs. P.'s table ignored her and went on with their own conversations.

Gylfie again turned to Soren and whispered in his ear, "You notice that Ezylryb and none of the other parliament members are here?"

Soren nodded.

"Well, big doings," Gylfie said, then blinked with one eye. Soren felt a surge of excitement. Gylfie must be onto something. Soren needed a distraction. Life had been, well, not quite the same since the appalling revelation that his own brother had trapped Ezylryb in the Devil's Triangle. And his own brother had vowed to kill him. Soren spent entirely too much time remembering those dreadful images of Kludd flying off, his face molten as the hot metal mask melted, screaming, "Death to the Impure! Death to Soren!" *My own brother. My very own brother is Metal Beak and he wants to kill me.*

After breaklight, the owls departed the dining hollow and made their way back to their respective hollows. Outside the great tree, the blizzard lashed. The gale-force winds had turned the sky white. It had been on a night like this in the thick of a blizzard that Soren, Gylfie, Twilight, and Digger had first arrived at the great tree. Now as soon as the four friends and Soren's sister, Eglantine, were alone, Gylfie spoke in a low voice.

"As I said to Soren at breaklight, something big is going on."

"How do you know?" Digger asked.

"Not one of the parliament members was in the dining hollow. There's an important meeting taking place."

"Getting ready for war, I bet!" Twilight said. "I'll bet they'll put us each in charge of a division."

"It's not war, Twilight. Hate to disappoint you," Gylfie said.

Twilight *was* disappointed. He loved fighting, and with his amazing quickness and ferocity, Twilight had proved that he had no equal.

"No, no war," repeated Gylfie. "It's higher magnetics."

"Oh, for Glaux's sake," Twilight growled. "How boring. As if we don't get enough of HM, as she now calls it, from Otulissa all the time."

"It's important, Twilight. We have to learn about this stuff," Digger said.

"That's just the problem," Gylfie said in a low hiss. "This stuff is spronk."

"Spronk?" the three other owls said at once.

"What's 'spronk'?" Soren asked.

"Spronk is forbidden knowledge," said Gylfie. There was a deep silence in the hollow.

"Forbidden knowledge? No, Gylfie," Soren said, "You have to be wrong. Nothing is spronk in the Great Ga'Hoole Tree. That's just not the Guardians' way. They would never forbid knowledge. They only want us to learn."

"Maybe not forbidden forever, but at least some things are spronk for right now," she replied.

"Well, I don't like it," Soren said firmly. "I'm completely against things being declared spronk."

"Me, too," Twilight said.

Digger blinked and then in that slow way he had of speaking when he was considering a problem, he said, "Yes, I think it's awful when they keep knowledge from young owls. Just suppose that Otulissa had not been permitted to read that book about the Devil's Triangle. We might never have been able to free Ezylryb."

"I think we should go tell them that this is all wrong," Eglantine spoke up for the first time.

"Before we do anything," Soren said now in a firm voice, "I think that we have to find out for sure."

"To the roots, Soren?" Gylfie asked.

"That's how you found out, isn't it, Gylfie?" Soren asked.

Gylfie nodded. She was a bit embarrassed, for this was an acknowledgment that she had been engaged in the less-than-admirable activity of eavesdropping on the parliament.

Thousands of inner passages wound their way through the Great Ga'Hoole Tree and, some months before, Gylfie, who often had trouble sleeping and would rise for a wander through the tree, had discovered a place deep in the roots where there was a strange phenomenon. Something happened to the timber at a certain point so that the sounds coming from the owl's parliament chamber resonated within the roots. Entering the root structure itself was a challenge, for the roots were huge and tangled, but Soren and his friends had found an ideal place where they could listen.

"Oh, I'm so excited!" Eglantine was nearly hopping up and down. "I've heard you talk about going to the roots but I've never been there. I've been dying to go."

There was a sudden silence as the other four owls exchanged glances. "You're not thinking of leaving me out. You better not leave me out. No fair!" Eglantine said in a desperate voice.

"I'm just not sure, Eglantine," Soren said. "I mean, first of all you would have to promise not to tell Primrose." Primrose, a Pygmy Owl, was Eglantine's best friend, and she told her everything.

"I won't, I won't, I promise. Listen, if it hadn't been for me, none of this stuff with higher magnetics would have started," Eglantine said.

This was true. If it hadn't been for Eglantine, who had been captured by the Pure Ones, imprisoned in the stone crypt of a ruined castle, and exposed to the destructive powers of the flecks, none of this would have ever happened.

"Well, all right," Soren finally said. "But not a word of this to anyone. Promise?"

"Promise." The young Barn Owl nodded her lovely heart-shaped face solemnly.

CHAPTER FOUR

Sprink on Your Spronk!

I cannot believe that teaching young and impressionable owls about such matters can really be helpful in the long run. Higher magnetics is a strange business. We ourselves have only begun to understand it all." Dewlap, the Ga'Hoolology ryb, was speaking.

The five young owls were perched among the roots, listening to the parliament's debate. Soren was ready to explode. Of course, higher magnetics was a strange business, especially compared to Ga'Hoolology, which was one of the most boring studies and chaws of the Great Ga'Hoole Tree. Ga'Hoolology was important, for it taught the processes of the tree itself and how to best keep the environment healthy and thriving, but it was also dull.

In this debate, Dewlap and Elvan, another ryb, were on the spronk side while Ezylryb and Bubo, the blacksmith at the Great Ga'Hoole Tree, were on the antispronk side. Strix Struma was undecided. Suddenly, the five young owls were aware of another presence. They felt a shadow slide over them in this darkest of places within the tree, and they froze. Then all of them together flipped their heads around. It was Otulissa!

What was she doing here? Soren was furious. *Racdrops!* he thought. Then Twilight beaked silently the words they were all thinking. "This really frinks me off!" "Racdrops" and "frinks" were two of the worst curse words an owl could say. There was only one worse — *sprink,* but no one ever said that. Not even Twilight. Say these words in the dining hollow and you were out in a flash. But Otulissa seemed unrattled. She merely lifted a talon to her beak to warn Twilight not to make any noise. Soren settled back down. There was absolutely nothing he could do about this now. They might as well just listen as the debate continued.

"Higher magnetics is not a science," Dewlap was saying. "It's dark magic, one of the shadow arts. And that book, *Fleckasia and Other Disorders of the Gizzard,* says as much, and must instantly be removed from the shelves."

"Wrong!" a voice boomed and sent the roots quivering so hard that little Gylfie nearly fell from her perch. It was Ezylryb speaking. "First, with all due respect, Dewlap, I must take issue with the term 'dark magic.' You use it in a derisive manner, as if something that is dark is negative. How can darkness in our world of owls ever be thought of as negative, something less good? For is it not in darkness that we come alive, that we rise in the night to fly, to hunt, to find, to explore, to defend, and to challenge? It is in darkness that our true nobility begins to bloom. Like the flowers that open to the sunshine, we open to the dark. So let us hear no more of such expressions as 'dark magic.' It is neither dark, nor is it magic. It is science. A science that we do not fully understand."

"All right, we need an explanation, Otulissa!" Soren demanded when they were back in the hollow. "You followed us. Who gave you permission?" But Otulissa cut him off.

"Who gave you permission to eavesdrop?" she shot back.

"Well, no matter," said Soren. "How come you're following us around?"

"I have as much right to as anyone. I don't want to be left out. I flew with you to rescue Ezylryb. You know that's true. And who was it who figured out the Devil's Triangle? Tell me that. And who knew about mu metal? Tell me that. Not to mention the fact that it was I who knew that fire destroyed magnetic properties. So who has more right to know about higher magnetics?"

Now it was Digger who stepped forward. "You," he

29

said simply. Otulissa breathed a sigh of relief. "And," he paused, "I honestly don't believe that one owl has more of a right than anyone else to know something. Isn't that what our objection to this whole spronk thing is about — our right to know? We should all be able to know." A stillness had fallen on the group. "Now, tell us, what do you think is spronk about higher magnetics, and why don't they want us to know about it? What are they scared of?"

"I don't know really. I think it probably has something to do with," she hesitated, "well, with what happened to Eglantine after the Great Downing — to her mind, to her gizzard."

"Was that different from what happened to Ezylryb?" Soren asked.

"Yes, I think so. Ezylryb just lost his sense of direction. He couldn't navigate, but Eglantine . . ." Otulissa turned to Eglantine.

"I couldn't feel. I was like stone — like the stone crypts they kept us in," Eglantine said.

"So why don't they want us to know about this?" Soren asked.

"I'm not sure. Maybe because they don't know that much about it themselves," said Otulissa.

"So," said Soren. "What do we do about all this?"

"We need to confront them," Twilight said. "I'm not

much for book learning, but I don't like the idea that someone can tell me I can't learn something. Makes me want to learn it all the more."

"But if we confront them," Gylfie said, "we're back to that same old problem again."

"What's that?" asked Otulissa.

"The last time we listened in at the roots and found something out and wanted to say something about it, way back last summer, well, we couldn't because then we would have had to admit that we had been eavesdropping, and we would get into really big trouble," said Gylfie.

"Hmmm," Otulissa blinked her eyes shut and kept them that way while she thought a moment. "I see the problem." Then suddenly she opened her eyes. The amber light in them flickered with a new brightness. "I have an idea. Remember that book they were talking about, that book that had to be removed from the shelves — *Fleckasia and Other Disorders of the Gizzard?*"

"Yes," Soren replied.

"Well, what if I go to the library and ask the book matron to fetch it for me? Then we'll see what happens. This will be a test case, so to speak," said Otulissa.

The other owls looked at one another. Otulissa was smart. And this was a very good idea.

So it was planned that as tween time neared, when the last drop of the day's sun began to vanish and the first shadows of twilight gathered, they would all go to the library and Otulissa would request the forbidden book. Of course, they would not go in all at once. Soren and Gylfie would already be there, and Otulissa would arrive with Eglantine and Digger. It was decided that Twilight would not be there at all because he seldom was in the library. Now Soren wondered if Ezylryb would be there, for he often was. What would he say when Otulissa requested the book?

The whole idea of forbidden books sickened Soren. At St. Aggie's, all books were forbidden. Entry into the library was not permitted for any owl except Skench and Spoorn, the brutal leaders of the academy. Academy! What a name. No one had learned anything there except how to become a slave and stop thinking.

Soren and Gylfie could hardly concentrate on the weather charts they were studying in the Ga'Hoolian weather atlas. Ezylryb was in the library, his usual uncommunicative self, sitting at his special desk. The only sound that came from that desk was the crunching of the dried caterpillars that he munched while he read. He was the most inscrutable of owls and only rarely revealed anything that could be called emotion. Yet Soren was drawn to him. He loved the old Whiskered Screech because it was Ezylryb who had first looked upon him and seen him as more than a young orphaned Barn Owl, more than just an owl scarred by the horrors of St. Aggie's. Ezylryb had seen Soren as a real, thinking owl who knew things not only through books and the information that the rybs taught, but through his gizzard. Gizzuition was, according to Ezylryb, a kind of mysterious thinking beyond normal reasoning, by which an owl immediately perceived the truth.

Gylfie gave Soren a nudge. Soren looked up. Otulissa had just entered the library with Eglantine. And suddenly, Dewlap had appeared behind the circulation desk with the book matron. Soren felt his gizzard turn squishy. He saw Otulissa's feathers droop as an owl's feathers do when he or she feels fear. She seemed to shrink. But then Soren watched and saw a fierce glint in the amber of her eyes. Otulissa's feathers seemed to puff up slightly and she flew the short distance between where she had stood and the desk. "Book Matron, would you be so kind as to look for a book that I can't seem to find on the shelves?"

"Certainly, dear. What is the title?"

"*Fleckasia and Other Disorders of the Gizzard.*"

Complete silence fell upon the library. It loomed up as

thick as fog on a humid summer night. Soren lifted his eyes toward Ezylryb, who was staring directly at Dewlap. His gaze bore into her like two fierce points of golden light. The book matron stammered, "Let me go see if I can find it."

"Oh, no, Book Matron," Dewlap said. "That is one of the books that has been temporarily removed from the shelves until certain decisions are made by the parliament."

"Removing books? Decisions? Since when are there decisions about books I want to read?" Otulissa drew herself up taller. Her feathers were now fully fluffed up. Otulissa's plumage was puffed to a degree that was most often associated with a posture of attack. She looked huge.

"There are plenty of other good books for you to read, my dear," Dewlap said in a soft voice.

"But I want to read *that* book," Otulissa replied. She paused a second. "Strix Emerilla, one of my distinguished ancestors, the renowned weathertrix, who has written several books on atmospheric pressure and weather turbulations, mentioned it."

Dewlap interrupted her. "The book you have requested has nothing whatsoever to do with weather."

"That's possible. But you see, Strix Emerilla had a wide-ranging mind, and I think that she mentioned this book as referring to a possible connection between gizzard disorders as related to atmospheric pressure variations."

"So?" Dewlap said.

"So, I have a wide-ranging mind, too. Now, please, may I have the book?"

Glaux bless Strix Emerilla, Soren thought. If anyone had ever told him that he would be blessing Strix Emerilla, whom Otulissa brought up whenever possible, he would have said they were completely yoicks.

"I'm very sorry, my dear, but that is absolutely impossible. That book has been declared temporarily spronk," Dewlap said primly and turned to the list she had been making.

"SPRONK!" Otulissa gasped. There was such emotion in her voice that every owl in the library looked up in genuine alarm.

"Yes, spronk." A testy note had crept into Dewlap's voice.

"There is nothing more ordinary, less noble, more ignoble, less intelligent, more common, and completely vulgar than spronking the written word," Otulissa sputtered. "It is completely lower class."

"Well, the book is spronk," Dewlap growled.

Then Otulissa swelled up to twice her normal size. "Well, SPRINK ON YOUR SPRONK!"

CHAPTER FIVE
A Mission Most Dreadful

S he fainted? Dewlap actually fainted?" Twilight said
with stunned disbelief.

"Yes, they rushed her to the infirmary," Soren said.

Soren, Gylfie, Twilight, Digger, and Eglantine swung
their heads toward Otulissa, who stood very still except
for her quivering beak. "I don't regret a word. Not even the
you-know-what word. I shall not apologize. Spronking is
very lower class, and it is against everything that the
Guardians of Ga'Hoole are and everything they stand for. I
don't care if I get a flint mop for this. I don't care if I get
chaw-chopped."

The other owls blinked in horror. To be chaw-
chopped was not simply a flint mop, which was the owls'
form of punishment. It was the ultimate humiliation that
could befall an owl of Ga'Hoole. It meant being dropped
for an indefinite period of time from one's chaw.

The five owls had returned to their hollow after the
episode in the library. Otulissa had come, too. They peered

at her now in awe and wonder. This very prim and proper owl had not only said the worst curse word in the owl vocabulary, but she had spat it at a ryb. What would happen to her? They could only imagine.

Suddenly, the parliament matron poked her head into the hollow.

"The lot of you are required in parliament immediately!" She did not sound pleased. "Except for Eglantine — she can stay."

Oh, Glaux! they all thought.

"Why don't I get to go?" Eglantine asked in a quavering voice. "I want to be included."

"You want to be included in a flint mop?" Twilight asked. "The last flint mop we got, if you recall, was having to bury pellets for Dewlap for three days. You were excluded from that, too, and believe me, you were lucky."

As the owls made their way down to the parliament hollow, Gylfie muttered, "Good Glaux, we're going to be burying pellets from now until summer."

"You didn't say the word, I did," Otulissa muttered. "It just sort of came out. I was amazed myself." But then she quickly added, "But I'm still glad I said it!"

Secretly, they were all glad she had said it. There was something terribly wrong with this whole idea of spronking. It did not fit in Soren's mind with the values of Ga'Hoole. *It is a sprinky kind of thing,* Soren thought. *Yes, good for Otulissa!*

When they were ushered into the parliament chamber, Dewlap was not there. Only Ezylryb and Boron and his mate, Barran, the two Snowy Owls who were the monarchs of the tree, were in attendance. And much to Soren's surprise, two other members of the weather chaw, Ruby, a Short-eared Owl and the best flier in the chaw, and Soren's flight partner Martin, a tiny Northern Saw-whet.

What's going on here? Why Ruby and Martin? Soren blinked at them in dismay, and they seemed equally puzzled as to why they had been called.

Barran coughed several times to clear her throat and began to speak. "The seven of you have been called here for a reason." Dread swam in all of their gizzards. What was it to be? Burying pellets? Or would they be chaw-chopped?

Boron was now speaking. "The seven of you combine an interesting array of talents." He paused. "As was proven in the extraordinary rescue of Ezylryb." Ezylryb nodded and seemed to fix his gaze on Soren. "Some have come to refer to you as 'the Chaw of Chaws.'" Soren almost gasped, and he felt his gizzard give a thrilled little twitch.

"To get to the point," Boron continued, "your special

talents as the Chaw of Chaws are now needed." One could have heard a blade of grass drop in the parliament hollow.

Glaux, Soren thought, *if Twilight pipes up about war and battle claws, I'll smack him.* That's all the Great Gray ever thought about. But of course he was brilliant in battle.

Then it was as if Barran had read Soren's thoughts. She swung her head around and fixed Twilight with a piercing stare. The light from her yellow eyes was like sharp, bright golden needles. "In a sense, it is much more dangerous than war. Although the stakes are as high, for you could be killed."

Whether Soren and his friends drew a breath for the next several seconds was questionable.

"Your mission is to penetrate the St. Aegolius Academy for Orphaned Owls."

What! Soren thought. *Go back!* He and Gylfie were horrified.

The two owls almost fell off the parliament perches. They were being asked to go back to the place that had attempted to destroy their personalities and their wills through the brutal processes called moon blinking and moon scalding.

"We have reason to believe that a dangerous group of owls, the ones that call themselves the Pure Ones, have possibly already infiltrated St. Aggie's with the intention of capturing the immense stores of flecks. We have had intelligence reports from Ambala that suggest this," said Boron.

"Ambala?" Digger said. "Isn't that where the slipgizzle was, the Barred Owl?"

"*Was* is right," Boron said. "As you know, he was killed. Over the last several months, we have been cultivating a new slipgizzle. She is rather frail and quite eccentric. They call her Mist, and she is perfectly suited for this work because through some odd accident, an almost terminal shock to her gizzard, she has lost all her coloration. Her feathers have turned a pale, almost foggy gray. Some might think she is a scroom. But she isn't. She does not fly well, but she has incredible powers of observation. The reports she has been sending about the Pure Ones are most disturbing."

Soren blinked. "Why?"

"They want flecks," Barran said, "and St. Aggie's has the largest repository of flecks in existence. But Mist thinks their interest extends beyond the flecks, and that is what we want you to find out. The two greatest threats to the owl kingdoms are St. Aggie's and the Pure Ones. The very idea of their being brought together in some sort of grand mischief is . . ." Barran hesitated. ". . . gizzard-chilling, to put it mildly."

Then Boron resumed. "So, you see how important the

seven of you are. We have faith in you. Now the question is, will you accept this mission?"

The owls were stunned. They had come in expecting a scolding or a flint mop and, instead, they had been charged with this important mission. Soren felt Ezylryb's gaze upon him. And Boron began to speak. "Soren and Gylfie, we realize that going back to St. Aggie's will be most difficult for you."

"Yes," Soren said slowly. "But, Boron, won't they recognize us?"

"Never!" Barran said quickly. "You were an owlet when you were there before. Your flight feathers had not fledged, nor had your face fledged white, and you were half your size. Gylfie — you, too, looked quite different."

"And," Ezylryb began to speak for the first time, "as you two well know, they are stupid, these owls of St. Aggie's." He paused. "But still, you'll need a cover story."

"A cover story?" Martin asked.

"Yes, where you came from, why you are there," said Ezylryb.

Otulissa raised her talon now to speak. "Can we say something like we got sick of the Great Ga'Hoole Tree? We didn't trust the Guardians — something like that."

"No," snapped Ezylryb. "They'll never believe you. It will raise their suspicions if they think you have anything to do with the great tree. You need to come from a place that they know very little about."

Soren suddenly realized that Ezylryb had thought out this entire cover story.

"A place like what?" Soren asked.

"A place like the Northern Kingdoms," said Ezylryb.

"Hold on a second." Digger had now raised a talon to speak. "Ezylryb, Gylfie and I are desert owls. The chances of our coming from the Northern Kingdoms are just about zero."

"I have it figured out," Ezylryb replied. *I thought so.* Soren blinked.

Ezylryb continued, but he did not stand still on the perch. He began sweeping through the air.

"Last summer, before certain unfortunate incidents like the Great Downing and my own entrapment in the Devil's Triangle, I had commenced a set of weather interpretation experiments. My original intention had been to pick up information on atmospheric particles and subparticles as they related to the displays we call the Aurora Glaucora, those magnificent colors in the summer sky when the entire night seems to pulsate with glorious lights. There was one last summer, as I recall, just around the time of my entrapment. Well, as often happens with scientific inquiry, one sets out to solve one problem and, quite by accident and happy surprise, one finds the answer to something entirely different. What I stumbled across was a new method for detecting distant williwaws."

"Williwaws!" Soren, Gylfie, Twilight, and Digger blurted out together.

"We know williwaws!" Gylfie said.

"Oh, you do, do you?" There was a churr, a kind of owl chuckle embedded in Ezylryb's voice.

"Yes, sir," Gylfie continued. "On our journey to the Great Ga'Hoole Tree, we thought we were right on course for the island when somehow we got sucked up into the Ice Narrows. . . ." Gylfie's voice began to dwindle off as the realization dawned.

Now Ezylryb really did laugh. "Aha!" he exclaimed. "You're getting the picture! Yes, you see, that's how desert owls get to the Northern Kingdoms. They get sucked up there. For what is a williwaw but a sudden violent wind?"

"He is so clever!" Otulissa said, her voice drenched in awe.

"Winds become confused. It is essentially a thermal inversion anomaly. Or, to make a long story short: You got your cover. You were sucked up, all of you, to the Northern Kingdoms," said Ezylryb.

"And then what?" Soren said.

Ezylryb stopped flying and lighted down beside Soren.

"Yes, and then what? Perhaps Gylfie and Digger, due to your desert background, did not find this cold place comfortable. And you other five, you felt that there was too much clan warfare going on. One clan chief fighting against another. Very disorganized. Disorganized is a key word to use with the St. Aggie's owls."

"Oh, yes!" Gylfie exclaimed. If there was one thing that St. Aggie's prided itself on, it was organization and efficiency.

Ezylryb continued. "You must say that you find clans an inefficient, cumbersome method of social and military organization." The old Whiskered Screech paused. "But if you just mention the Northern Kingdoms, the land of the Great North Waters where I come from, every St. Aggie's owl will be intrigued. It is the last frontier to be conquered. If an owl has been there, every other owl is consumed with curiosity about what they have seen or experienced. And if you suggest that the Northern Kingdoms might be vulnerable, you shall be welcomed."

"But we can't fake it. I mean, we only got as far as the Ice Narrows. We don't know that much about Northern Kingdoms," Gylfie said.

"You will by the time I get through with you," Ezylryb said bluntly.

The seven young owls exchanged nervous glances.

Then Boron began to speak again. "The seven of you shall report to Ezylryb's hollow daily for the next week. During that time, Ezylryb will give you intense tutorials in the history and culture of the Northern Kingdoms."

Soren could sense Otulissa swelling with excitement over the prospect of yet another intellectual challenge.

"I cannot impress upon you too much the need for absolute secrecy. No one is to know about this mission. Talk of it must not go beyond these walls or the walls of Ezylryb's hollow," Boron said.

"What about our own hollow?" Soren asked. He was thinking of his sister, Eglantine. It would be hard to keep this from her. "And when we are with Ezylryb, won't the rybs miss us for our usual classes?"

"We've thought of that," Barran said. "In regard to Eglantine, we have felt, as I am sure you have, that your hollow is a bit crowded with five of you in there. Primrose is knocking about in that hollow of hers all alone since that one Masked Owl from the Great Downing died of summer flux.

"Primrose has asked time and time again if Eglantine could move in with her since they are such close friends. I think Eglantine would like to, but she felt that you might be hurt. In truth, I think that she would be more comfortable with Primrose, who is somewhat closer to her age. I shall handle her move. I'll tell her that we have discussed it with you, and you understand."

Barran then turned to Otulissa, Ruby, and Martin. "You three present another situation. We cannot go about moving everybody, or it will arouse suspicions. With your hollowmates, you will just have to be as discreet as possible.

"Now, as for your cover story for when you are gone . . . well, leave that to us. Ezylryb is devising a so-called scientific weather experiment that is going to require the transfer of some equipment to an area on the other side of the Sea of Hoolemere. The execution of this experiment necessitates the abilities of the members of a variety of chaws. Right, Ezylryb?"

The old Whiskered Screech nodded.

Boron continued, "I think that just about does it, then. You are dismissed for now, but please expect to report to Ezylryb directly at tween time for your first history lesson on the Northern Kingdoms."

The seven owls started to leave the parliament hollow. "Just one moment, young'uns," Ezylryb called out. "I have something here for Otulissa." She blinked and turned toward her chaw leader. "I believe you were looking for this?" In his three-taloned foot that had been mangled in an ancient battle, Ezylryb held out the book *Fleckasia and Other Disorders of the Gizzard.*

Otulissa gasped. "Really?!" She blinked in disbelief as he extended his talons with the forbidden book.

"Yes . . . really, Otulissa. And I quite agree with you — sprink on spronk."

Barran gasped and Boron winced. But they said nothing as the sound of the vulgar word pealed through the hollow.

CHAPTER SIX

Learning by Heart and by Gizzard

There is the Hollow of Lyze, on Stormfast Island, that is Ezylryb's clan. Then there is the Hollow of Snarth on the Tridents, a cluster of three small islands. Then there is . . ."

Ruby made a deep and mournful noise halfway between a sigh and a sob. "I'll never learn all this history. There are so many clans and so many islands that I can't keep straight what's in the Kielian League and what's in the league of the Ice Talons. It's just too much."

Otulissa had, of course, learned all the dynasties of the Northern Kingdoms, the great battles, the heroes, and the villains. She had memorized passages from the long narrative poem the *Yigdaldish Ga'far* that related the heroic adventures of the Great Snowy Owl Proudfoot and an Eagle Owl named Hot Beak. The others felt positively dim in comparison, especially Ruby, who was not much of a scholar and had trouble sounding out some of the words in the books Ezylryb provided. She claimed that certain words got stuck in her throat. "These words are like rocks. They sound like gagging."

Soren felt that Ruby had a point. The words were hard to say, and many did have harsh, gagging sounds. But he suddenly had another thought.

"I'm not sure if we should know all of this stuff so well. It's not as if we were hatched and raised in the Northern Kingdoms. Remember, we just arrived accidentally, thanks to a williwaw. It might seem weird if we know all this history like we were . . . were . . ."

"Grot-ghots?" Otulissa said. "That's the Northern Kingdom term for native."

Soren and Gylfie blinked at each other. *Unbelievable, this Spotted Owl,* thought Soren. *Does she ever let up?*

"I think Soren is absolutely right," Digger spoke up. "How are we supposed to have learned all this stuff if we were just blown off course? As a matter of fact, Otulissa, you're going to have to watch yourself."

"Watch myself?" She blinked rapidly. "How do you mean?"

Twilight stepped up close to her and bobbed his head forward. "He means put a mouse in it!"

Otulissa looked crestfallen. "Oh . . . oh," she said softly.

"I see what you mean. Yes, they might think we were grot-ghots and not merely blown off course," she paused. "I've learned so much, though."

"Well, you'll be able to use it sometime, I'm sure, Otulissa," Soren said. He actually felt a bit sorry for her. "And I think we can tell them a lot about the military stuff that Ezylryb mentioned. I mean, Ezylryb did say that we were supposed to pretend that we found some sort of weakness. How did he say it, Gylfie?"

"He said that we must say something to the effect that we find the clans an inefficient and cumbersome method of social and military organization. Remember, St. Aggie's owls have never been to the Northern Kingdoms, so they're going to believe what we tell them." Gylfie paused. "But you know what is even more important for all of you to learn? The most important lesson of all."

"What's that?" asked Martin.

Gylfie looked across to Soren and blinked. Soren knew what was coming. "How not to be moon blinked."

When Soren and Gylfie had been snatched by the owls of St. Aggie's, they were shocked to find owls who no longer slept during the day. In a complete reversal of the normal cycle, these young owls were forced to sleep at night. Furthermore, during the nighttime, they were periodically awakened and made to perform the sleep march under the glare of a rising moon. It did not take Soren and Gylfie long to figure out that the reason for the march was to make hundreds of young owlets rotate through the moon's glare. And no one was allowed to stay in the safety of the shadows for too long. For among older owls it was known that to sleep with one's head exposed to the bright-ness of the moon's light, especially a moon at the full shine, had a peculiar effect on the gizzards and the minds of owls, especially young impressionable ones. Through some mysterious process, their own personalities began to disintegrate, they lost any sense of their uniqueness, and their will simply evaporated.

To aid in this process, they were each assigned a num-ber in place of their name. While marching, they were told to repeat their old name endlessly. A name, or any word, repeated endlessly breaks up into meaningless sounds. It is no longer a name. It is just a senseless collec-tion of noises. So Gylfie and Soren had pretended to say their names while marching, but instead, they had re-peated their assigned numbers. Thus their numbers be-came meaningless, not their names.

Soren and Gylfie had developed other tricks as well. Some were riskier than others. But the most effective strategy of all in resisting moon blinking had been to silently whisper the legends of Ga'Hoole. At that time in Gylfie's and Soren's lives they had thought they were only repeating stories. They had no idea that the Great Ga'Hoole Tree really existed, and that the stories were true. By repeating these tales, Soren and Gylfie were able to resist moon blinking and even moon scalding, which was far more damaging.

So their work in teaching the other owls these ruses began in earnest. Each owl was given one or two stories of the Ga'Hoolian cycle to remember and retell in a whisper to themselves and to one another. It was Soren's belief that if one knew the story well enough, one did not have to say the words out loud. The story began to live within them, within their gizzards until each owl became a guardian of his or her story.

Ruby found remembering the stories of Ga'Hoole much easier than sorting out and remembering the clans of the Northern Kingdoms. Since Ruby was the best flier of the group and a superb collier, it was her task to be the teller of the stories that were about forest fires. These were called the Fire Cycle.

Twilight, of course, was the teller of the War Cycle. Gylfie, as a member of the navigation chaw and thoroughly knowledgeable about the stars and the constellations, told the stories of the Star Cycle. The Star, the Fire, and the

War cycles were the three main cycles. The rest of the stories were of weather, heroes, and villains. Otulissa, Digger, and Soren divided these up among themselves. They were the stories on which owls grew strong and bold. They were stories to be learned by heart and by gizzard.

CHAPTER SEVEN
A Special Flint Mop

It was the day before the mission. As the light grew dusky, the seven owls began to stir. They were all nervous and slept little during that day. The three owls who did not share a hollow with Digger, Gylfie, Soren, and Twilight were especially jittery. It wasn't easy being alone in one's hollow with only a couple of other owls who knew nothing of the mission you were about to embark upon. One was completely isolated with his or her thoughts and fears. A sense of dread inevitably began to creep through each owl's gizzard. *Will I do my part? Will I remember my section of the Ga'Hoole cycle? Will I be moon blinked? Moon scalded?* Or perhaps even worse, would they be discovered and then subjected to some brutal punishment, such as the one called laughter therapy, in which feathers were plucked from an owl's wings?

Ruby looked enviously at her hollowmates, another Short-eared and a Great Horned Owl, as they snoozed, their sleep smooth as summer air, undisturbed by any thoughts of wing pluckings or moon scaldings. In her head she kept repeating the saga of the famous collier from ancient times. The words that opened this story of the Fire Cycle sang softly in her head.

It was in the time of the endless volcanoes. For years and years in the land known as Beyond the Beyond, flames had scraped the sky, turning clouds the color of glowing embers both day and night. The volcanoes that had been dormant for years had begun to erupt. Ash and dust blew across the land and, although it was thought to be a curse from Great Glaux on high, it was something else. For this was the time when Grank, the first collier, was hatched. This was the time when a few special owls discovered that fire could be tamed.

And in another hollow, Martin repeated to himself a short piece from the weather sagas about an owl that, just as Martin once had, plunged to the bottom of the sea to be rescued, not by a seagull as Martin had been, but by a passing whale.

Otulissa tried to sleep, but she had failed, as had the others. Her head now swirled with so many thoughts. There was so much to know, to learn — and to *un*learn! Soren had been right. She couldn't appear too knowledgeable about the Northern Kingdoms. And then there was her portion of the Ga'Hoolian cycle to know, which one could never learn well enough. On that her very life, her gizzard, her mind depended.

There was no sense even trying to sleep, she thought. She untucked the book Ezylryb had given her from where she had stashed it deep in the moss and down of her nest bed. She would read just one or two pages. Reading did ease her mind. It always had, always would. She was just about to turn the page when suddenly a voice oozed into the milky light of the hollow.

"Caught you!" Otulissa's gizzard seemed to drop to her talons. It was Dewlap. The Burrowing Owl had poked her head into the hollow through the sky port, blocking the mid-afternoon sun, so that shadows spilled across the floor. She beckoned with a talon at the end of her long, feather-less leg. "Come here, immediately, and bring that book!"

"B-b-b-but, but . . ." Otulissa stammered.

"No buts."

Otulissa got up shakily and moved toward the sky port. Dewlap snatched the book.

"But you don't understand," Otulissa said. "Ezylryb . . ."

"I understand perfectly. More than you think. Now, you follow me, missy. I have a special flint mop for you."

Otulissa didn't know what to do. She could hardly tell Dewlap that within two hours she was supposed to go to the cliffs on the far side of the island to meet the others for a top secret mission. She knew that Ezylryb was fast asleep in his hollow, and it was always strictly forbidden to wake him up. What would happen if she simply refused to fly after Dewlap? But that, too, might raise a fracas. In no way could she jeopardize the mission. It was unthinkable. So the Spotted Owl followed the old Burrowing Owl. And as she followed her, she could not help but notice what a miserable flier this ryb was.

Burrowing Owls, of all the owls, were the least skillful and the weakest fliers. They were known, however, for their superior abilities in walking and even running over all sorts of terrain on the ground. Dewlap was the worst flier Otulissa had ever seen. She lacked silence and balance as she flew. Her strokes were rough and feeble. She rarely got any significant lift from them and when she carved a turn, it was a complete mess. And she was attempting to fly while still holding in her talons the book she had snatched from Otulissa.

Otulissa thought she knew where Dewlap was leading her; to another side of the island, about as far away as could be from the cliffs from which they were supposed to take off on their mission. This was a favorite flint-mop site. The cliffs here were not very high. There was a small beach below, where seaweed drifted up, sometimes accompanied by dead fish or pellets yarped by owls as they flew over Hoolemere. The dead fish, the pellets, and the seaweed were extremely rich in nutrients that benefited the tree if properly buried at its base. So groups were often sent on collection trips. This was obviously the flint mop that Dewlap had selected for Otulissa.

Well, Otulissa thought, *perhaps if I work quickly, I can get it over with and still be on time.* But before she even began, Dewlap insisted that Otulissa go kill a vole for her, as she was hungry. The young owl did this promptly and dropped it at the Burrowing Owl's talons, which were placed protectively on the book.

"That's a nice vole," Dewlap said in that oozy voice of hers. Otulissa did not respond. "You're a bit angry, I suppose." Otulissa would not even give her the satisfaction of looking at her. She immediately flew down to the beach and began collecting seaweed and salt-soaked pellets.

The sky had turned a dusky purple. It was a weak light at the end of one of the short, winter days. The world would soon enough be plunged into darkness. In the winter, First Black seemed to drop suddenly and sharply like a stone blade from the sky, severing the day from the night, the light from the dark. Six owls waited on the cliffs.

"She was supposed to be here at tween time!" Soren muttered. Then for perhaps the tenth time, his voice betraying his anguish, "Where could she be?" He almost moaned. "Otulissa, of all owls! She's never late, always prompt."

"I'm sure she'll be here," Martin said, although there was little conviction in his voice.

How long can we wait? Soren wondered. The winds were growing confused. It was hard enough flying across the Sea of Hoolemere from this particular point. It lengthened any journey across the sea and the winds were very often unfavorable, as now, and they were getting stronger. Soren and Gylfie were soon going to decide whether to go or not, with or without Otulissa. The Barn Owl and the Elf Owl had been appointed the leaders of this mission since they were the only two owls in the group who had actually been inside St. Aggie's.

They exchanged glances.

Gylfie blinked. *I think we have to go.*

Soren could read the thought in the Elf Owl's eyes. *She's right*, he thought.

"Prepare to fly!" Soren gave the command. "Course check, please." He turned to Gylfie.

"North by northeast, keeping wingspans between the first two points of the Golden Talons and the starboard foot, turning to east after three leagues, then due south. If possible, keep to starboard of the Little Raccoon, which should be rising soon."

"Fly!" Soren hooted in the shrill screech of a Barn Owl.

Meanwhile on the crescent beach, Otulissa muttered

to herself, "What am I going to do?" She had collected a huge pile of nutritious debris. It would require at least four trips to take it all back to be buried at the base of the tree. And Dewlap kept sending her out to fetch snacks.

Just now she called down to Otulissa, "Dear, I'm feeling a twinge of hunger. I just saw a chubby little ground squirrel wander by. Do you suppose . . . ?"

Suppose what, you fat old witch? But Otulissa dropped a dead fish in the pile and flew up. One of the things that really frinked Otulissa off about Dewlap was not just her voice but how she pretended to be so polite — all the "Dear, do this" or "Dear, do that" or the "Would you minds." Everyone knew there was no choice. Why did she even bother with this pretense of sweetness?

In the moment that Otulissa spiraled down in a dizzying plunge to kill the ground squirrel, the blade of darkness had begun to fall. And with a quick slash, day was severed from night and the world turned black. A small animal died, and Otulissa rose, her beak bloody from killing. *They've gone!* she thought mournfully. She power-stroked through the confusing winds that had grown stronger toward Dewlap, who was perched on a rock outcropping, her talons still clutching the book. Otulissa started to angle in to drop the squirrel at the Burrowing Owl's long, ugly legs. But then something seized her. There

60

was a tremendous lurch in her gizzard. Indignation flooded every hollow bone in her body. She flung the bloody ground squirrel directly into the face of Dewlap. "SPRINK ON YOU!" she cried.

Then in the buffeting tumultuous winds, Otulissa peeled off over the Sea of Hoolemere.

"You come back here this instant! You, you — !" Dewlap spluttered. She spread her wings and attempted to launch herself from the rock outcropping onto the heaving billows of wind. But she was soon windmilling her wings in a most unseemly fashion, ricocheting off maverick drafts and becoming drenched by the building seas whose white spume swirled now like scrooms in the night. As she lashed out in futile desperation against the tumult, against the wind and water, the book *Fleckasia and Other Disorders of the Gizzard*, which she had left on the rock, tumbled end over end into the sea.

CHAPTER EIGHT

Across the Sea and to the St. Aegolius Canyons

"Owl to downwind." Twilight had just caught sight of an owl emerging from a thickening fog bank.

"Great Glaux! It's Otulissa!" Soren hooted in amazement. The other owls spun their heads to look. Their beaks dropped open in utter surprise at what they saw. Power-stroking against a strong headwind was Otulissa, a fierce scowl in her eyes, her beak set in an angry clamp. In another few seconds she had banked, turned, and glided into the windward flanking station, her usual flight position in the Chaw of Chaws.

"Sorry I'm late," she said.

"What happened?" Soren asked in a stunned voice.

"You won't believe this, but Dewlap caught me."

"Caught you? How?" Gylfie asked.

"Caught me reading a book, the book that Ezylryb gave

me. She made me do a flint mop." Otulissa paused. "Well, I did it for a while."

"And then what?" Gylfie asked.

"I threw a dead ground squirrel in her face and flew off. So here I am."

"You what?" Ruby said.

But Soren cut in, "Now see here. We have to keep flying and we must keep our minds on our business. These winds are getting worse. Otulissa can explain it all to us when we fetch up on the other side. For now, keep flying. Gylfie, give us a course check."

"Two more degrees of easterly, then turn due south."

Good, Soren thought. Turning east would put the wind just off their tail quarter and ease their flight. They wouldn't be working against it so much.

The plan had been simple. After turning south, they would be on a direct course for The Beaks. Heading west and skirting the coastline of The Beaks, they would enter the mouth of the River Hoole, flying straight upriver until it joined a tributary that flowed out of Ambala. They would then fly across the southern portion of Ambala, still heading west, and onto the far border of the St. Aegolius Canyons, where they would fetch up for the next day. It would make for a long night, but since it was winter, the dawn would be slow to break, and therefore there would be no danger of crow mobbing in the daylight hours. They would then wait until the following evening when they would make their approach and entry into the St. Aegolius Canyons where, at the very center, St. Aggie's lay deep in a stone maze of chasms, jagged gulches, shadowy clefts, and ravines.

Where they had fetched up for the day the woods were thin, and in the distance they could see the stone spires of the St. Aegolius Canyons etched against the horizon. Otulissa had just finished her story. The owls were in awe of the Spotted Owl. She was known for her ferocity of wit and intellect, but not for such unseemly outbursts, and never ones that involved raw power. Imagine, flinging a bloody ground squirrel into the face of a ryb!

"Glaux knows what flint mop awaits you, Otulissa. A major one, no doubt," Gylfie sighed.

"I know," said Otulissa solemnly. "But I'm still glad I did it."

Soren clattered his beak a couple of times, a habit that he had developed when he was thinking hard, as he was now. He didn't like what he had heard. He found it disturbing that Dewlap had used Otulissa to serve her, literally having her go out and hunt for food. That did not seem right. He also felt that this could provide a major distraction for the seven of them. He did not want the Chaw of Chaws thinking about flint mops for some boring old owl.

"You know," Digger began to speak slowly. "I don't think there will be a flint mop for Otulissa."

"Why not?" Ruby asked.

"Well, think about it. Major flint mops have to be approved by the parliament. So for her to receive one, Dewlap is going to have to explain too much," said Digger.

"You're right!" Gylfie said suddenly.

Digger continued, "Dewlap would have to tell Ezylryb that she tried to take away a book that he had given to Otulissa. She would also have to admit that she had been asking Otulissa to hunt food for her while on this flint mop. I mean, the whole thing is not going to put Dewlap in the best light. She's going to appear as exactly what she is — a tedious old owl who went against the most revered ryb of the entire tree. I don't know about you, but I wouldn't want Ezylryb against me. I would much rather have Dewlap against me and Ezylryb on my side than the other way around."

Soren breathed a sigh of relief. What Digger had just said made perfect sense. Now the owls would not be distracted by thoughts of flint mops. They were all very tired from their long flight, which had been mostly against headwinds. They were ready for sleep, and soon they were all snoozing peacefully.

Except for Soren and Gylfie. They were still wide awake and discussing the strategy for their entry into the St. Aegolius Academy for Orphaned Owls.

"I think we should go to the Great Horned entrance," Gylfie was saying. "I remember Grimble once talking about how mature owls, owls like himself, always came through the Great Horned entrance." Grimble, a Boreal Owl, had been captured as an adult by St. Aggie's patrols and held as a hostage with the promise that his family would be spared. He was a strong fighter. That was why Skench, the Ablah General of St. Aggie's, and Spoorn, her first lieutenant, had wanted him. But Grimble had been imperfectly moon blinked, and something in him responded to the plight of Soren and Gylfie. He taught the two young owlets how to fly so they could get away. On the harrowing night of their escape, Grimble had died, murdered while trying to help them go free. Soren could not think of Grimble without a quiver in his gizzard and an ache in his heart. But he had to put all that aside now. Such feelings would only be a distraction. This mission was going to require everything that he and Gylfie had, plus more. They must successfully resist moon blinking, convince the owls that they had come to join the horrible evil that was St. Aggie's, and to gather the information that Boron and Barran desperately needed in order to preserve peace in the owl kingdoms.

Boron, Barran, and Ezylryb had been very precise about the kind of information they needed. First, the Chaw of Chaws must determine if any of Kludd's followers, the Pure Ones, had infiltrated St. Aggie's. If so, were they sneaking flecks out of the library, where the flecks were stored? Second, they were to find out if the rulers of St. Aggie's had learned anything more about flecks. Previously, they had known hardly anything. When Skench had burst into the library as Gylfie and Soren were about to escape, it was only her ignorance that saved them. The Ablah General had not known to take off her metal battle claws and full battle regalia before entering, and she, pulled by magnetic force, slammed into the wall of the library where the flecks were kept.

Although it was tempting to stay together once they were in St. Aggie's, Soren and Gylfie knew that this was not the best strategy. To achieve their goals, the group would have to separate and spread themselves throughout the academy. There were many divisions, including the pel-letorium, the hatchery, the eggorium, and the battle claw repository.

Finally, toward noon, as a dim winter sun hung in the sky, Gylfie and Soren fell asleep. The short days of brief light would afford them only a few hours of rest before the sky would begin to darken and it would be time for them to rouse themselves and face the unthinkable — the return to the most dreadful place on earth: St. Aegolius Academy for Orphaned Owls.

CHAPTER NINE

The Most Dreadful Place on Earth

Below them, the landscape began to bristle with rocky spires and needles.

"I've never seen anything uglier," said Martin, who came from the wild and gloriously green forest of Silverveil. Silverveil was a forest where immense trees hung with ivy and were clad in a thousand different kinds of moss, where oceans of ferns trembled in the ground breezes, where streams made their own sweet music as they laced their way through ancient, wooded lands. Some said that the forests of Silverveil were so beautiful that it was as close as a living owl could ever get to Glaumora, the owl heaven, without dying.

Whereas St. Aggie's might be the closest an owl could get to Hagsmire, the owl hell, without dying. Soren scanned the rocks below, looking for the Great Horned entrance. This entrance was an immense boulder that perched precariously on an outcropping and was said to resemble a Great Horned Owl.

"All right, ready?" Soren asked the six other owls. They all nodded. They lifted off and headed for the boulder of the Great Horned entrance. As they approached, two Long-eared Owls lifted off the two peaks, the horns of the boulder, that rose against the colorless winter sky.

"Here they come," said Gylfie quietly. It wasn't Jatt and Jutt, two St. Aggie's warriors, for they had been slain in the desert more than a year ago when they had attacked Digger. But it was the Long-eared Owls who had always served as the main guards at St. Aggie's.

Now these two owls banked and came up in a flanking maneuver, one on each side of the seven owls' flight formation.

"You are flying into a no-fly zone. This is the territory of St. Aegolius. You are now under our escort. You break formation under risk of severest penalties. You shall proceed with us into the interrogation crevice," said one Long-eared Owl.

"Yes, sir," Martin answered. They had decided that Martin would be the spokes-owl. Soren knew that both he and Gylfie had changed greatly since they had first been snatched and brought here as captives, but they did not want to risk the slightest chance that some owl might hear a familiar note in their voices or catch a recognizable glint in their eyes. It had been Soren and Gylfie's intention to fade into the background of the Chaw of Chaws and to do as little as possible to attract any attention at all.

"Steep bank to...uh...uh...this way," the other Long-eared Owl commanded.

Glaux, these owls don't know port from starboard! The thought exploded in Soren's mind and it gave him great joy. He realized how much he had learned since arriving at the great tree. It would be brains and not brawn that succeeded here, and this was a comforting thought.

Within a minute, they were sliding into the dense shadows of a deep crevice. Down, down, down they plunged, until they lighted on the gritty floor. Above, only a thin sliver of the sky was visible. There were enough bad things about St. Aggie's, but perhaps one of the worst was that in the deep canyons, stone wells, pits, and crevices, the sky seemed so far away. Oftentimes it was not even visible. In just a handful of places did the sky cut through. One of these places was the glaucidium and the moon-blazing chamber, where the horrible moon-blinking procedures were endured.

"Wait here!" one of the Long-eared Owls barked, and

then waddled off into a stone slit. Soren saw Twilight's and Ruby's eyes blink in wonder. *Get used to it*, Soren thought. *This is the world of St. Aggie's.*

It was a stone world riddled with seams, slits, and slots through which owls seemed to simply disappear. Soren was looking around when he sensed that Gylfie was quivering. He looked down and saw that the little Elf Owl had edged in closer to him. Her eyes were blinking open in a staccato rhythm. Emerging from another crack was a Great Horned Owl and it was none other than Unk, Gylfie's old pit guard! Surreptitiously, Soren extended one wing ever so slightly, so it barely grazed Gylfie's head. He felt her calm down. *We'll get through this, Gylfie. We are smarter than they are. We'll get through it.* He willed the words that took shape in his head to somehow get through to his best friend. He knew how scared she must be. He was terribly frightened of meeting up with Aunt Finny, the old Snowy Owl who had been his pit guardian.

Although the pit guardians were not considered the highest level of guards, there was something dreadful about them. They were, of all the owls of St. Aggie's, the slyest and the most duplicitous. They were masters of falsehood. They pretended to be warm, but it was all part of their strategy to suck a young owlet into their power.

But now it seemed that Unk was no longer a pit

guardian. His words, no longer jollied and honeyed, sliced the shadows of the crevice. "How did you come here? How did you know about us? What is your purpose?"

Martin took a tentative step forward. In a quavering voice he began. "My name is Martin." *Oh, racdrops!* Soren thought. *Why'd he have to say that?*

"Names mean nothing here. You shall be given a number designation. Someday you might earn a name. Until then, I repeat, names mean nothing. Continue."

"We came from the Northern Kingdoms."

A shiver seemed to pass through Unk and, at a slight, almost invisible signal, the other Long-eared Owl vanished through another crack. Hardly a minute had passed before a Western Screech stepped from the same crack, followed by an immense and ragged Great Horned Owl. It was Skench. Soren and Gylfie felt their gizzards almost split with fear.

"I am Skench, the Ablah General. I am told you come from the Northern Kingdoms — and yet two of you are desert owls. Now tell me how desert owls found their way to the Northern Kingdoms."

"Well, Your Ablah," Martin nodded in his most obsequious manner. And he began to tell the story they had concocted of williwaws and violent winds. Soren looked on with amazement. Martin was doing a magnificent job.

He even threw in the Lobeleian current, which the St. Aggie's owls knew nothing about, but they nodded wisely for they were too embarrassed to admit ignorance. In a brief time, Martin had laid the perfect groundwork with his cover story. The Chaw of Chaws appeared smart, but not too smart. They were owls who had seen a lot of the world and become disenchanted with the Northern Kingdoms. Although they had not known one another before they had been sucked up into the Northern Kingdoms, they found that they had shared their dislike for the place. "The clan system doesn't work," Martin said.

"Not for racdrops!" Twilight added.

"There's no real leader. Everything's in a constant state of confusion," Martin said.

"Yeah," Twilight said with just the right mixture of gruffness and meekness. "We want a real leader. We are humble owls."

Great Glaux, he's overdoing it! Twilight — humble? Soren tried to imagine such a thing. But here he was, the Great Gray dipping his head submissively to Skench. And most incredible of all, Skench was buying it!

"This is all very interesting," Skench said, turning to Spoorn, who had emerged from another crack in the canyon wall while Martin was speaking. "These owls will all need to be debriefed, and then we shall decide on their number designations and their work assignments. But first they must begin the processes of the glaucidium."

By "processes of the glaucidium," Skench meant moon blinking. Soren now hoped fervently that the owls remembered all that Gylfie and he had taught them about the strategies of resistance.

Already the other five owls had begun remembering their portions of the Ga'Hoolian legend cycle. Ruby began to think of Grank and the time of the endless volcanoes. She pictured the first collier flying high over the exploding cone of the volcano and fielding the fiery debris that scored the sky. Twilight thought of the Battle of the Tigers that happened in the time of the long eclipse when the huge cats that roamed the world in those ancient days went yoicks from lack of sun and began a murderous rampage. It had been a Great Gray named Long Talon who had plunged down from the black one night and killed their leader — a tiger one hundred times his own size.

The Chaw of Chaws was ready. Ready with their legends burning feverishly in their brains, ready with their courage, ready to fight the evil that was held in this dark, shadowy, skyless place. Their blood boiled, their wits were keen, and their hearts grew bold.

CHAPTER TEN

To Fear the Moon

The moon had dwenked, and the nights were completely black. It would be four days until the newing began. Then the first faint glow of moon would appear like the thinnest white strand of down, a mere wisp. But each night it would grow fatter and more brilliant. They would hope for cloud cover, but the skies in the St. Aegolius Canyons were usually clear, as it rarely rained. Their mission, of course, had been planned with this in mind. If they arrived near the end of the dwenking, the Chaw of Chaws would have four dark nights before the moon would, as it began once more to fatten and grow bright, batter their exposed heads, dull their brains, and make still their gizzards. These four days would give them some time to figure things out.

It was different being an almost mature owl as opposed to an owlet, as Soren and Gylfie were when they had last been at St. Aggie's. There were only two stone pits for newly arrived larger owls, whereas there were least a dozen pits to accommodate the hundreds of owlets. Four members of the Chaw of Chaws were together in one pit, and three in another. Twilight, Soren, and Ruby were in a stone pit watched by an Eastern Screech who had just received his name, Mook, and had dispensed with his number. He was quite full of himself, strutting around snapping commands and making dire threats about the consequences of asking questions. *Wh* words — *what, why, when, where,* or any question at all — were strictly forbidden at St. Aggie's. But that did not prohibit Skench from calling the seven owls out of their stone pits at various times day or night to ask them endless questions about the Northern Kingdoms. During these sessions, Soren noticed Otulissa's struggle to contain her vast knowledge of those kingdoms and their ways.

Soren had been given the number 82-85. He couldn't remember what his previous number had been. He did remember, however, his old pit guardian Finny, or Auntie, as she had insisted on being called. She had turned out to be the most brutal owl Soren had encountered at St. Aggie's. He dreaded meeting up with her again.

Finny had caused Hortense's death. Hortense was the most courageous owl Soren and Gylfie had ever met, but when they had first arrived, it appeared that Hortense was the most perfectly moon blinked of all the owlets. Her number had been 12-8.

Odd, Soren thought. He could remember Hortense's number and not his own. It had turned out that she was not an owlet at all, but a fully mature Spotted Owl, small for her years, with slightly crippled wings. And she was a double agent. Assigned to the hatchery as a broody, she had been sneaking some of the eggs snatched by St. Aggie's patrols and delivering them secretly to two huge bald eagles who returned them to the forest kingdoms — in some cases, the very nests from which they had been taken. But then she had been discovered. From a split in the rock where Soren and Gylfie hid, they had witnessed the terrible battle that had raged between one of the eagles against Finny, Skench, Spoorn, Jatt, and Jutt. They could not see it all, but they could hear the horrendous fight. Soren would never forget the voice of Hortense growing dimmer and dimmer as she fell from the high outcropping, pushed, they knew, by Auntie. And then Auntie's words in her cooing voice, "Bye-bye, 12-8, you fool." The last two words had become a snarl that scalded the night.

Oh, Glaux! Soren did not want to see Auntie ever again.

But that was not to be the case.

Four days passed. Then came the first evening of sleep marches. Along with the hundreds of newly snatched owlets, the older owls were herded into the glaucidium. Each member of the Chaw of Chaws knew by heart and by gizzard his or her own saga of the Ga'Hoolian legend cycle. They knew, perhaps not as well, the sagas of others. Martin stood near Soren and looked up at the newing moon.

That I would ever fear the moon? Martin thought. *How extraordinary!* He tipped his head up. There would be new constellations in this part of the world, for they were far to the south of Hoolemere and the Island of Hoole. He had learned about these constellations in navigation class with Strix Struma, the navigation ryb, but had never actually seen them or traced them with his wing tips as they did in class with her.

It did not seem long before the sleep alarm sounded and the owls were required to march.

Just as Soren and Gylfie had warned, the owls were told to repeat their names as they walked. But the Chaw of Chaws very quietly did just the reverse — they repeated their numbers. This was perhaps the easiest part of their resistance strategy, for there was such a babble of voices that no one really knew what anyone else was saying. If a sleep monitor did come near the owls, each had a fake name that he or she would say for that moment.

"Albert!" Soren blurted out as a monitor approached. It was a Boreal Owl with dim yellow eyes.

"Excellent, excellent," the Boreal Owl said as he lighted down next to the block of owls that Soren had been grouped with for the sleep exercises.

When he passed by, Soren resumed repeating his number very quietly. He did not want to attract anyone's attention, especially the Barn Owl two rows in front of him. Soren had planned to move his way up toward that Barn Owl. Every Barn Owl in St. Aggie's, except possibly the ones that had been snatched as owlets, was suspected of being an undercover agent, a slipgizzle, for the Pure Ones. And this was perhaps the most important part of their mission: to find out if the Pure Ones were infiltrating St. Aggie's.

"Halt!"

Great! Soren thought. He was right next to the Barn Owl.

"Assume the sleeping position!" The head sleep monitor barked from an outcropping several feet up from the floor of the glaucidium. Hundreds of owls instantly stopped repeating their names and tipped their heads back so that the small scrap of moon shone down on them. Soren stole a glance at the owl next to him as the beginning of his portion of the Ga'Hoolian legend cycle began to whisper in his head. His gizzard seemed to tingle with delight.

Flint was the Barn Owl's name. Soren had heard him say it right before the halt was called. But now Soren had a disturbing thought. If Flint was an infiltrator, how was he supposed to resist moon blinking? What use would a moon-blinked owl be to Kludd and the Pure Ones? He would have to discuss this with Gylfie when he got a chance. He stole a glance at Flint. How could he tell if this owl was an infiltrator? He was a Tyto alba, which was the only possible clue. But not all Tyto albas belonged to the Pure Ones, and certainly very few believed this ridiculous notion of owl purity. Well, Soren could not think of that right now. He must remember his part of the Ga'Hoolian legend cycle. He had chosen the very same saga that he had repeated when, as a young owlet, he and Gylfie had been taken to the moon-blazing chamber to be scalded by the light of the full moon. It was the one that began "Once upon a time, before there were kingdoms of owls, in a time of ever-raging wars, there was an owl born in the country of the Great North Waters and his name was Hoole...."

CHAPTER ELEVEN
Flecks in the Nest

Now that their first moon blinking had occurred, the owls in the Chaw of Chaws were considered ready to be assigned to their first task. Soren was bitterly disappointed that he had not been sent to work in the pelletorium, or at least the inventorium, for these places would have provided him with the most access to activities connected with flecks. Instead, he had been assigned to the eggorium, along with Martin. Ruby had been assigned to the hatchery as a broody. Gylfie was in the pelletorium, which was good because she knew her way around there. Digger was in the inventorium along with Otulissa, and Twilight was in the armory — a seemingly perfect match. He was to learn how to polish the battle claws.

As they were about to enter the eggorium, Soren turned to Martin. "Nothing I can say, Martin," he whispered, "can really prepare you for what you are about to see."

Martin gulped. Soren had told him about the hundreds upon hundreds of eggs that patrols from St. Aggie's snatched from nests to bring to their own hatchery and raise in captivity. Soren had said that one of the worst things he had ever witnessed was a hatching of an owl chick at St. Aggie's. It was loveless, unnatural, despicable, and cruel. Martin gave a little gasp now as hundreds of white eggs of all sizes glistened in the dark. But then he felt Soren freeze beside him. A scarred old Snowy had waddled up to them. One of the Snowy's eyes wept continuous tears. It was cloudy so that its yellow color seeped out pale and foggy. There was a nasty gash that ran down her face and across her beak at a steep angle. It had healed jagged, and the scar was very black in the stark white feathers of the Snowy's face. It appeared to Martin like a bolt of lightning in reverse — black on white.

But despite the mangled face, Soren would recognize this owl anyplace. It was Finny.

"Call me Auntie," she spoke now in a creaking voice as she inclined her head toward them. She had an odd smell about her. Soren wasn't sure what it was. But now Soren saw that the reason her voice creaked was that there was another large gash like a black necklace around her throat. He hadn't seen her after the terrible battle on the outcropping when the eagle had tried to save the egg that Hortense was delivering. *Great Glaux,* thought Soren. *Finny might have killed Hortense, but the eagle certainly did a job on Finny.*

Is she looking funny at me? he wondered. *Does she recognize me?*

"Another Barn Owl," she was saying. "Well, we can use them. Got a passel of Barn Owl eggs." She then explained the procedure for sorting the eggs according to their types. Soren was familiar with this and although his gizzard was quivering madly, he managed to pretend to pay attention and nod as she explained that they were to look for eggs of their own species and roll these eggs into a designated area.

Martin and Soren's plan was to do their work so well as to be promoted to the position of moss tenders. Being moss tenders would give them greater range of movement. They would not only spend time in the eggorium, but in the hatchery where Ruby, as a broody, was sitting on a nest. Soren and Martin worked hard and efficiently for several hours, rolling egg upon egg to the designated areas.

"82-85! Report to main station," a Barred Owl had come up to Soren and, in the hollow tones of the truly moon-blinked, had issued this command. Soren's gizzard stirred and then gave a joyful little leap as he saw the Barred Owl head in the direction of Martin and repeat the same command. *Maybe we've been chosen!* he thought. *Maybe this will lead to something.*

None of the seven had yet discovered anything substantial about Barn Owl infiltrators. They had their suspicions, but so far there wasn't any real evidence.

"82-85 and 54-67." Auntie stared at them. The jagged scar gleamed darkly on her face. "You have proved yourselves efficient as egg sorters. You shall now be permitted to work, on occasion, as moss tenders. You shall begin tonight. With the additional duties, you have earned additional dietary supplements." She paused and Soren's gizzard turned squishy as the pale light in her eye hardened. "My sweeties, you may have a bit of vole. I think it will be a treat. That will set you up just fine, dearies." And she gave Martin a little tweak with her beak. Soren saw him flinch.

Oh, Glaux, Soren thought, *it's the old Finny.* There was something even scarier about Finny when she was being all honey-beaked and charming because Soren knew it was false. And there was always a price to pay. She might slip you an extra piece of vole, or one of the plump rock rats that scurried through the canyons, but then you were expected to give her something in return — information, or perhaps to spy and report to her. That was the way it worked and, little by little, an owl dug himself in deeper, owing her more, making himself more vulnerable to her power, deceit, and brutality. Nonetheless, they had no choice now. This is what they had wanted and this is what they got. At least they would get to see Ruby in the hatchery. But it would not be until their third day as moss tenders that they would have a good opportunity to speak with Ruby.

"Moss tender! Moss tender! Attention, please!" It was Ruby. She was broody on a nest of Barn Owl eggs. There was never any attempt to match up the species of the broody with that of the egg. Therefore, Barn Owls might be sitting on Barred Owl eggs, or Short-eared Owls, such as Ruby, might be sitting on Great Gray eggs. It seemed that they tried their best to avoid matching up the broody with the type of eggs. Soren supposed it was because when an egg finally hatched, they didn't want the chick to have the least sense of anything familiar — like a true parent. Love was not part of hatching. These chicks were not supposed to love; they were supposed to obey.

"I was just there," another Barn Owl said. "You don't need anything more."

"Oh, I just thought a nice fat worm would do. Don't you worry about it. There's two moss tenders right nearby," Ruby said, looking in Soren and Martin's direction. "One has a worm in that wad of moss. And the other, I know, will fetch me that rat from the crack over there where I just saw the tail of one disappear." Martin blinked, for he did not have a worm in his moss. Soren had been next to the crack, and he hadn't seen a rat disappear into it.

He and Martin had managed a few fleeting conversations with Ruby before the end of this third day as moss tenders. But this was the first time that she had actually called them over. The previous day she had been sitting on Spotted Owl eggs. But they had hatched out, and she had been assigned to a new nest.

The other Barn Owl seemed relieved to not have to fetch anything for the broody. Broodies were treated well. They were constantly being offered a great array of delicacies and nutritious foods that the other owls hardly ever saw.

"I have to make this quick!" Ruby spoke in a whispery hiss. "Listen! They're doing something funny to the nests of Barn Owl eggs."

"Who?" Soren asked.

Ruby nodded toward two Barn Owl moss tenders who were tucking in bits of moss and dry grass into some nests on the far side of the hatchery.

"What do you mean?" Soren asked. Oh, the sound of those *wh* words were like honey in his beak. He could almost taste them!

Ruby stirred in her nest. "Shield me so they won't see."
It was strictly forbidden for a broody to climb off her nest,
but now Ruby moved to one side. Because she was such a
superb flier, she was able to loft herself very quickly into a
low hover inches above the nest.

Martin and Soren gasped. Deep amid the woven twigs
and grasses of the nest were three eggs. Between them, in
the strands of moss, glinting fiercely, were small sparkling
bits.

"Flecks!" Soren said.

The truth suddenly broke upon Soren like a clap of
thunder. There were infiltrators. They had somehow escaped being moon blinked. They had gained control of at
least some of the flecks — but why were they weaving
them into the moss that they poked into the nests? What
could flecks do in a nest with unhatched eggs? Soren felt
his gizzard grow still and cold. *They're doing something dreadful,* he thought. *I am sure! I must get to Gylfie. Racdrops! If only
we were in the same pit!*

And there was still so much of the day left. It would be
hours until tween time, when they could return to their
pits.

"And there's another thing," Ruby said. "It's worse."

Soren couldn't imagine what could be worse.

"You know that old Snowy Owl down in the

eggorium — Auntie Finny?" Soren nodded. "You know how she has kind of a weird smell about her?"

Soren nodded again. "But how would you know that? She's not up here in the hatchery."

"She comes up here a lot. She's an egg eater!"

"What?" Soren and Martin asked.

"Yeah, I think it's easier for her to sneak them up here than in the eggorium. She does it just before a new broody has been assigned to a nest, and not only that, she eats hatchlings — the ones that aren't quite perfect."

Soren and Martin were dizzy with nausea. Their gizzards twisted painfully, and they both thought they might yarp.

CHAPTER TWELVE

The World According to Otulissa

Otulissa was counting the bits of bone, teeth, feather, fur, and flecks picked from the owl pellets in the pelletorium and placing them onto trays in the inventorium. She had been working there for several days with Digger and two other owls. When the trays were filled, they were taken for storage in the library. But she, Digger, and the other two owls — a Barn Owl and a Whiskered Screech — were not permitted any farther than the entrance to the library. Once there, they would hand over the trays to Skench or Spoorn, the only owls allowed in the library.

Otulissa and Digger wanted to know more about this library, which was so heavily guarded. Was it just because the flecks were there and Skench and Spoorn didn't want them stolen? But that didn't exactly make sense. Flecks slipped away all the time from the inventorium. Otulissa had figured this out just the night before. She had not yet been able to tell Soren. But this Barn Owl, 92-01, while on duty, had slipped some to another Barn Owl. Otulissa was sure 92-01 was an infiltrator, and she planned to watch her closely. But watching wasn't enough. Otulissa had become a master of disguising questions as statements in order to extract information. She and Digger had planned a small dialogue between the two of them that they hoped would encourage the two other owls to contribute some information.

Digger yawned elaborately. "I could use a good leg stretch. You know, a Burrowing Owl like myself never minds a long walk. I wish that they'd allow us to go into the library, if only to exercise. What a shame it is forbidden."

"It has always been strictly forbidden except for Skench and Spoorn," Otulissa added, knowing perfectly well from Soren and Gylfie that this wasn't completely true.

"Not always," said 92-01. *Ah, it worked!* Otulissa thought at once. The statement was drawing out an answer to a question unasked. "Once there was a fracas, I am told. An owl who had betrayed Skench and Spoorn was killed, and Skench, through some strange event, was made powerless."

"Powerless!" exclaimed Digger. "It is almost impossible to think of the Ablah General as becoming powerless."

"Yes, almost yeep," said 92-01. When an owl went yeep, its wings seemed to lock. It lost its instinct to fly and would suddenly plummet to the ground.

"Unthinkable," Otulissa gasped in awe.

92-01 seemed pleased that she had so impressed this snooty owl. *What does she have to be snooty about after all?* the Barn Owl wondered.

But she was soon to find out. For it was as if Digger and Otulissa silently read each other's minds.

All right, Digger thought, *time for you to show off what you know, Otulissa. Gently, gently.*

"Yes, almost yeep," 92-01 continued. "It's hard to think of, I know. But it really wasn't yeep, mind you. It was magic."

"Magic!" Otulissa exclaimed. "No, I don't think it was magical at all. It was higher magnetics, probably a typical higher magnetic reaction."

The Barn Owl blinked. It was clear to both Digger and Otulissa that she was dying to ask a question. Otulissa took pity on her and fed her just a bit more. "Yes, if Skench had been wearing diamagnetic materials, it wouldn't have happened."

"Wh" — 92-01 clapped her beak shut on the nearly escaping question. "How interesting," she said instead. She looked almost in pain as she tried to contain the unasked question.

Later, after Digger and Otulissa had finished their work, they were able to talk in private on their way back to their stone pit.

"I was pretty excited for a while there with 92-01," Otulissa was saying. "But where did it all lead? We're no closer than before to knowing why the Barn Owl is sneaking flecks out, and what is going on in the library with the flecks. Where is she sneaking them to? How would the Pure Ones get them? We need to talk to Soren. Too bad there are no sleep marches now," she said.

The moon had dwenked again, and it would be another two days until they could meet up with the other owls in the glaucidium when the moon-blinking process would begin again. In the meantime, they were allowed to sleep in their stone pits.

Otulissa was startled when, in the middle of a very pleasant dream of swooping through a verdant forest on the track of a plump vole, she was nudged gently by her stone pit guardian. He was a large oafish Great Gray who liked his charges to call him Cubby. In the tradition of all the pit guardians, he was always promising Otulissa extra treats.

"Sweetie, I hate to wake you. You were sleeping so nicely. I promise I'll have something good and fat and bloody for you when you return. But my dear, right now — and this is quite an honor" — He hunched his shoulders up as if he were just tickled to death about what he was going to say next — "Who do you think wants to see you?" Then he giggled raucously. "Oh, sshhh! Don't tell — I let slip a question, didn't I? Well, you won't tell."

Glaux, Otulissa loathed this creepy owl. "Of course, I won't," she answered.

"Good girl," he whispered. "But I'll tell you — Skench, the Ablah General."

Otulissa blinked with surprise.

"This is quite an honor, I would say," he continued. "Follow me."

Otulissa followed the Great Gray through the narrow corridors and stony slots of St. Aggie's Canyons. St. Aggie's was a place made for walking more than flying. With its narrow corridors and endless skinny passageways, it was nearly impossible to spread one's wings. The air always seemed dead, for nary a breeze stirred so deep in this rockbound place. And when one was required to fly, it was usually straight up from the ground with powerful wing flaps. St. Aggie's was a perfect prison for young owlets with undeveloped flight skills.

Skench and Spoorn's cave perched high on a cliff. Otulissa had never been there before, but she had heard talk of it. Now Cubby led her into a wider space and began to spread his wings. His span was immense as all Great Grays, and the wafts of air shook the comparatively small Spotted Owl. Otulissa decided to take advantage of the moving air and launch herself onto its billows. It would be easier to gain altitude on these drafts than on the still, unmoving air. The two owls spiraled upward.

"This way!" the Great Gray flipped his beak over his shoulder and called to her. A pale rose-colored stone needle projected horizontally out from the cliff, piercing the air. Two Great Horned owls stood as guards. They nodded to Cubby and Otulissa as they lighted down.

What could Skench and Spoorn possibly want with me? Otulissa wondered. *Not more about the Northern Kingdoms, and never before in their cliff cave. Every other time it had been down in one of the pits.*

"Enter!" a voice commanded.

Otulissa stepped into the cave and blinked. A white, heart-shaped face seemed suspended in the dim light of the cave.

"I would like you to meet Uklah," Skench said.

Otulissa blinked again, this time in confusion. Uklah? It was 92-01, the Barn Owl, the infiltrator.

"Uklah is her new name," Skench continued. "When she came here, her name had been Purity. You know all that nonsense about the Pure Ones."

Uklah snorted derisively at this. "Never heard such nonsense in my life."

Now Otulissa was thoroughly confused. She had thought that 92-01, or Uklah, was a spy for the Pure Ones. But whose side was she on?

"I can see you're confused, 45-72." Spoorn tipped her head toward Otulissa, her yellow eyes set off by the unusually pale circular swirl of gray feathers across her brow.

"You thought I was a spy," Uklah churred softly as owls do when they find something funny or amusing. "Well, I was when I originally came."

"There are several here," Skench added. "Oh, we know who they are. All Barn Owls. We're very suspicious of 82-85, that Barn Owl you arrived with. All Barn Owls immediately fall under suspicion. The Pure Ones are dying to get at our flecks. They want to take over the St. Aegolius Canyons."

Otulissa swung her head between Skench and Uklah. *What is going on here?* she wondered. *Is she or isn't she a spy?*

"But I saw Uklah sneak flecks out," Otulissa said.

"Of course you did," Skench answered. "She can't have

her fellow spies think she's become a turnfeather. Uklah feeds them just enough information, some true, some false, so they won't become suspicious of her. The flecks she sneaks out are tucked into nests by the spy moss tenders in the hatchery, the nests with Barn Owl eggs. We retrieve them during shift changes. There are two other Barn Owls who work as double agents up there. They pull out the stolen flecks for us. So there's no harm done."

Otulissa was dying to ask what harm they had been expecting. But she had to guess that putting magnetic materials into nests with eggs could cause a major disturbance in the gizzards or the brains of unhatched chicks. Even though Dewlap had seized the book, she had read enough of the beginning chapters of *Fleckasia and Other Disorders of the Gizzard* to know that overexposure to flecks at certain periods in a young owl's life was not a good thing. And Soren had told them about how that brave owl Hortense had felt that the reason she was so small for an owl of her age was due to the large deposits of flecks that run through the creeks of Ambala. Perhaps flecks in the nest would cause the Barn Owl chicks to resist moon blinking and to identify in some way with the Pure Ones.

Now Otulissa swiveled her head toward Uklah and carefully began to phrase her question as a statement. "Turnfeather to the Pure Ones," she began slowly.

"No need for that," Skench interrupted, sensing what Otulissa was about to do. "You can ask questions here. But not yet. We have some questions. Higher magnetics — what is it? Why, on that terrible night when those owls escaped more than a year ago, did I go yeep? It was the magic of higher magnetics."

"No, it wasn't magic," Otulissa replied. "It was science. Magic and science aren't the same thing. I don't know anything about magic. Higher magnetics is science."

"Tell us about it," Spoorn urged. "What makes us feel strange when we are in our battle claws around flecks? Where do flecks get their power?"

Otulissa was debating with herself just how much she should tell them. This was different from giving them information about the Northern Kingdoms. They could do real damage with what they might find out about flecks.

Uklah stepped forward. "There was a terrible battle in the woods," she said, "between the High Tyto, Kludd, and his brother, and owls from the Great Ga'Hoole Tree. Those owls did something to the bags of flecks that destroyed their power. What was it? We need to know."

That was when it clicked in Otulissa's mind. Owls like this did not need to know. They needed to be kept ignorant. She would feed them false information — just for a little while, just long enough so she could gain their confidence and the Chaw of Chaws could escape. As far as Otulissa was concerned, their mission was accomplished. They had found out what they had come to learn. There *were* infiltrators. A few, like Uklah, were double agents, actually working for St. Aggie's. The rulers of St. Aggie's didn't know much about flecks. The Pure Ones were planning to take over St. Aggie's but because of the double agents, they might be thwarted. It was time to get out.

But first Otulissa wanted to know something. She would be crafty about how she said it. "Although flecks in the nest of unhatched eggs will disturb the chicks' brains in a certain way, exposure for adults is quite different."

"Oh, yes! You are smart, aren't you! That's how we avoid being moon blinked. Small amounts of flecks ingested lessen the effects of moon blinking considerably," said Skench.

Just what I thought! Otulissa then continued. "Well then, of course, you know about flux density." The owls stared blankly at her. "You don't know about flux density? Oh, dear. Then I should begin at the beginning...."

Otulissa never mentioned that fire can destroy the flecks' power. She never told them that she had read that certain other objects that did not contain flecks could temporarily gain the magnetic powers of flecks by rubbing up against one another, nor did she tell them about mu metal, which could shield one from the powers of a magnetic field. But she did talk. She talked and she talked and she talked, as only Otulissa could talk. She made up something she called the Basic Fleckasian Laws of Moss, which were complete and utter nonsense.

CHAPTER THIRTEEN

A Rogue Smith Is Called

Deep in the ancient forest of Silverveil, there was a crumbling ruin of a castle. High in one of its few remaining turrets, in a stone notch, a scarred, ragged-feathered owl perched. He squinted through his remaining eye at the moon rising behind fast-moving, torn clouds. A storm was brewing. He turned his bare, horrid face toward the bitter wind. The Rogue Smith of the Silverveil would be arriving soon with his new mask. He had threatened the silly old Snowy Owl with death before she would agree to make him the mask, and then she claimed that the ingredients for mu metal would be hard to find. Nickel was scarce in these parts. She found it, however, after his Pure Guard lieutenant Wortmore had roughed her up a bit. But Kludd did not want to think about all that right now. He wanted to think about the idea that had begun to stir in him when he lay wounded in the hollow of the Brown Fish Owl, the idea of laying siege to the Great Ga'Hoole Tree with its secrets of fire and magnetics, its warriors and scholars. This notion had set his gizzard twitching and inflamed his brain ever since he had first thought of it. He would have no rest until he had captured the great tree.

Beneath him, he saw one of the Pure Guards spiraling up with a great Snowy Owl in its wake.

"His High Tyto!" the guard cried out. "The Rogue Smith of Silverveil has arrived."

The Snowy Owl appeared nervous, and the mask trembled in her talons as she clutched it.

"Enter the turret," Kludd spoke, without turning his face.

The two owls lighted down on the stone floor of the turret. The Rogue Smith of Silverveil placed the mask at Kludd's talons.

"Finest quality mu metal?" Kludd asked.

"Yes, High Tyto." The Snowy made an obsequious gesture.

It was common knowledge that all rogue blacksmiths were loners. They lived in caves and seldom consorted with other owls, except for matters of business — making battle claws, helms, shields, and the occasional bucket. A few acted as slipgizzles for the Great Ga'Hoole Tree. For even in their isolated states, they saw a great deal and could pick up information others might not have. Owls often became quite talkative as they were being fitted for battle claws. The Snowy, however, had never been tempted to become a slipgizzle, not in the slightest.

Now, as she worked fitting the mask to Kludd's horrendously mutilated face, she realized that this owl was different from any other owl she had ever encountered. He was absolutely silent. His silence was as dense as the metals the smith forged in her fires. But through this silence, the smith sensed some awful thing. She wished this owl would speak, would say something. She felt she had to know what this owl was planning. Snowy Owls have highly refined instincts for danger, weather, and certain kinds of celestial events. If what she sensed was true, for the first time in her life she was tempted to become a slipgizzle.

Finally, the Rogue Smith of Silverveil thought of something. She coughed once or twice. "I say, I have a new battle claw design. Some find it quite good. Light in battle, exceedingly sharp. If you would like one of your lieutenants to try them out, I would be happy to do a fitting over at my forge. No cost. You could have them on trial."

"Light, you say?" the High Tyto asked.

"Oh, yes — quite light, and a new kind of finely notched edge. Tears flesh beautifully." The smith could almost feel the excitement in the High Tyto's gizzard. "You know, of course, I learned my craft on the island of Dark Fowl," said the Rogue Smith of Silverveil.

The High Tyto interrupted her. "Dark Fowl in the Northern Kingdoms?"

"Yes, Sir . . . I . . . I mean, High Tyto."

"Wortmore! Get me Wortmore," Kludd called.

The Snowy's gizzard trembled a bit. The very owl who had been sent to rough her up was now being called to go back to her forge for a fitting.

The Rogue Smith of Silverveil tried to keep her own talons from shaking as she hammered the third metal talon on Wortmore's left claw to a tighter curve, so it would fit perfectly.

"The High Tyto and I are exactly the same size, you know. So what fits me will fit him." Wortmore was positively chatty now. He had even apologized for roughing up the Snowy. "But orders are orders," he had added. And he was a bit partial to Snowies, he had whispered.

Lovely, thought the smith. But she held her beak and managed to keep up her end of the chatter. "Now, if the High Tyto likes these, how many do you think he'll need?"

"Well, certainly enough for the Pure Guard, and there are eighty or more in that division."

"My goodness, that's quite a few."

"Oh, yes — and that's only the Pure Guard. We've got many other divisions, and by the time of the Great Massing, the size of that guard will be triple." Wortmore broke off as if trying to count.

"The Great Massing?" the Snowy asked.

"Yes, on Cape Glaux."

Cape Glaux! There was only one reason why owls would gather on the wind-battered cape that stuck out into the most turbulent waters of the Sea of Hoolemere. That was the quickest, most direct route to the Island of Hoole. It was risky flying for most birds, except the Guardians of Ga'Hoole themselves, and maybe eagles. And that was exactly what the Rogue Smith of Silverveil realized she must do right now. She must go to those two eagles of Ambala, the ones who lived with the strange Spotted Owl called Mist. She was a bit of a slipgizzle herself, and she might know something about this massing on Cape Glaux.

As soon as Wortmore had flown off, flashing his new battle claws in the moonlight, the Rogue Smith of Silverveil began to gather her few belongings. She had to find a new location, that was for sure. There was no way she was going to hire out to make claws for the Pure Ones. She had had a good run of it here in the ancient old forests, but she could set up her smithy someplace else. Ambala wouldn't be bad, especially since she was going there anyway, to find the eagles. She put her hammer, tongs, a few of the best examples of her work, and her metal box of live coals to start her fire into a sack made from the hides of red foxes that she had killed years before. She pulled tight the drawstrings and, clutching the bag in her talons, lifted into the night. She headed south by southeast, toward the corner of Ambala where the eagles roosted along with Mist.

CHAPTER FOURTEEN

Escape

Soren crept up onto the nest he was sitting in the hatchery. Underneath him there were three eggs that had been snatched from the nest of a Barred Owl in the Shadow Forests. It was a miracle that the members of the Chaw of Chaws were all in the hatchery, either as broodies or moss tenders. It had taken a lot of work, especially on Otulissa's part. They were all shocked when she had told them about the double agent. Over the course of a few days, she had been feeding Skench and Spoorn a steady flow of false information, and thus had gained many privileges for herself. Through a combination of her sly wit, privileged position, and still more false information, she had managed to procure all of them positions in the hatchery. And it was from the hatchery that they planned to escape.

It would have been better to escape at night, but the moon was full now, so they were required to be in the glaucidium for moon blinking, the effects of which they had all resisted through their strategy of concentrating fully on the cycle of legends of Ga'Hoole. And now in this dawn they were going to have to fight their way out. Remembering the legends would not help. They had only their talons, their beaks, and their powerful wings. If all really went well, they might be able to escape without too much of a fight. They had planned to create a distraction under the cover of which they would slip away. Soren tried to quell his fears. He had to remember that, unlike the first time he had escaped from St. Aggie's, he now knew how to fly. He and Gylfie had never really flown before when they had escaped from the library a year ago. Their wings had barely fledged, and the only way out of that library was straight up. Here in the hatchery it was still straight up, but there was a little bit more room to spread one's wings and gain a grip on the air.

Their plan was simple. As soon as Otulissa had told them about the double agent, Soren, Gylfie, and Ruby had begun to sniff out other spies. Otulissa had told them to watch out for the double agents — the turnfeathers — who were helping Uklah by taking the flecks out of the nests. When they had figured out which owls those were, they could launch their escape plan. Just two days ago, they had figured out who all the turnfeathers were. And now they planned to expose them. A major fight would break out. Barn Owl against Barn Owl. Agent against double agent. The blood would splatter, the feathers would fly. It was under this cover of blood and feathers that the Chaw of Chaws would escape.

Soren swept his head about in an almost complete circle. Everyone was in place. Martin, Digger, and Otulissa were plying the well-worn paths with their little bundles of moss and tucking them into the nests for cushioning and insulation of the eggs. Soren, Ruby, and Twilight were sitting on nests. Of all the owls, Twilight had been the most challenged by St. Aggie's. Independent by nature, proud of his experience in "The Orphan School of Tough Learning," St. Aggie's required just the opposite — complete submission, humility, and unquestioning obedience. Yet Twilight had proved himself to be a superb actor. Now, tonight he was going to be an actor no longer. It was Twilight who would instigate the fight by uncovering the turnfeather agents.

A Barn Owl moss tender was making his way toward the nest on which Twilight sat. It was one of the turnfeathers. *Perfect!* Soren thought. They had been waiting for just this opportunity: One spy had just put flecks in, and now another, a double agent, was ready to pull them out. Twilight would expose them both.

"You Barn Owls!" Twilight yawned and then a snarl

109

seemed to curl his voice. "Your pal over there, 78-2, was just here stuffing in new moss and now you're here taking it out."

A silence seemed to fall over the hatchery. "What did you just say?" the turnfeather asked, forgetting the rule of never asking questions.

"Hey, same thing over here," Ruby piped up. "Give a broody some peace. These Barn Owls . . ." She couldn't finish her sentence. The Barn Owl who had poked moss into Twilight's nest minutes earlier suddenly flew back across the hatchery. With a rake of her talons, she slashed the head of the double agent Barn Owl.

"Fight!" Twilight screeched.

In an instant, the hatchery was an explosion of feathers. At first, it was just Barn Owl against Barn Owl, and Soren himself had to dodge plenty of blows as he made his way up to the rim of the hatchery. But the owls who were not Barn Owls felt betrayed as well. So they joined in the fight. They didn't care which Barn Owl they attacked, for they were all spies and enemies of St. Aggie's.

Finny was now flying directly toward Soren. "82-85, you're in on this, too!" The voice creaked in the manner of huge, rotten-timbered trees in winter storms. The jagged scar, like a bolt of black lightning across her pure white face, flickered ominously.

"Got me a taste for Barn Owl, I do, I do." Now her voice seemed to seep out thickly with relish at the very thought of such a taste. Soren remembered that she had an appetite for unhatched eggs and freshly hatched chicks. He could smell it on her, and it made him nauseous. She was advancing directly on him now, her talons spread for attack, her beak pulled open.

"Egg eater!" Soren screamed, and dodged in flight. She kept coming. The sweet nauseating stench rolled through the still air of the hatchery. Soren felt a slash to his tailfeathers as another owl flew by and struck him from the rear. He saw specks of blood fly through the air. Finny was backing him into a corner. There would be no flight space. She was twice his size! Suddenly, a voice rang out, a rhythm seized the air. It was Twilight. A taunt blistered the hatchery as the Great Gray flew straight in toward Finny.

> *Oh, Auntie this and Auntie that,*
> *You ain't nothing but a white-feathered rat.*
> *One-two-three-four,*
> *I got something else in store.*
> *Five-six-seven-eight,*
> *You're about to meet your fate.*
> *Nine-ten-eleven-twelve,*
> *Oh, great Glaux, you sure do smell!*

A special place for egg suckers like you,
Yeah — you'll make a tasty stew!

Auntie had gone into a yeeplike daze. She drifted to the ground, her eyes glazed in a kind of fascinated terror as Twilight danced in the air above her. Soren flung out his talons, toppled her over, and rose in flight. "Let's get out of here!"

"Wait," Twilight cried. "I haven't finished. I feel another verse coming on."

"Are you yoicks?" screamed Otulissa.

"Come on, Twilight!" Gylfie swept by and then suddenly Finny seemed to regain her senses. She stared at Gylfie, reached out with one talon, and knocked the little Elf Owl flat. Gylfie trembled in a corner as the huge and now truly enraged Snowy Owl came toward her.

"I know you, I know you!" she kept saying. "And I know your friend there, too, 82-85, except that Barn Owl was 12-1 when he was in my pit before."

Soren, hovering above, could not believe what he was seeing. Auntie had now reached out to grab Gylfie by the throat with her talons. Without thinking, Soren folded his wings and, with a breathtaking velocity, plunged downward. The force alone sent Finny sprawling. A dusty blur flew upward. With one rake of his talons, Soren opened the old scar on the Snowy's throat. The pure white feathers ran red.

"Behind you, Soren!" Otulissa called.

It was Skench. "So, you are an imposter! The owl who escaped from the library," she screeched. Spoorn was soon there, too, along with three other immense Great Horned guards. Four against one. A taunt from Twilight wouldn't be enough. It was hopeless. This was the end for Soren. He could only hope the others would go on without him. They had to save themselves. They had to!

But at that moment, just above him, he heard the voice of Gylfie. "Once upon a time before there were kingdoms of owls, in a time of ever-raging wars, there was an owl born in the country of the North Waters and his name was Hoole. This is the first legend of Ga'Hoole and how that great tree came to be. You see, some say there was an enchantment cast upon this owl called Hoole at the time of his hatching."

Skench and Spoorn and the other two owls stopped. Their wings fell to their sides. If they had been flying they would have plummeted to earth, but they were yeep standing up. *Gylfie is doing just what we did in the moon-scalding chamber reciting this, the most powerful of all the Ga'Hoolian legends,* Soren thought. *Look at them flinch each time the word Hoole or Ga'Hoole is uttered!*

Soren's voice now joined that of Gylfie's. "This owl called Hoole was said to have been given natural gifts of an extraordinary power. But what was known for certain of this owl was that he inspired other owls to great and noble deeds. Although he wore no crown of gold, the owls knew him as a king. In a wood of straight tall trees he was hatched, in a glimmering time when the seconds slow between the last minute of the old year and the first minute of the new year, and the forest on this night was sheathed in ice."

Ever so softly, Soren flapped his wings and rose in the dawn light. He kept reciting the first legend, the one known as the Coming of Hoole.

And then they were gone — seven owls faded into the breaking day. St. Aggie's was behind them. Ahead lay the great Forests of Ambala, then due north were The Barrens, then turning two points east of north was Silverveil, out across the Bight to Cape Glaux, then straight over the Sea of Hoolemere to the island of Hoole and the Great Ga'Hoole Tree.

CHAPTER FIFTEEN
An Old Friend Discovered

A small lake glittered in the sunlight of the crisp winter morning. The seven owls were flying over Ambala but it was too dangerous to continue in the broad light of day. They could be mobbed by crows. And although Soren's tail had stopped bleeding where it had been slashed, it was painful. It felt like the shaft of one of his tail feathers had broken off. Whenever Soren tried a ruddering maneuver with his tail feathers, it hurt, and his turns were sloppy. He spotted a large sycamore below that grew at the edge of the lake.

"Prepare to land, sycamore below," Soren called.

The owls began to bank. Soren wobbled as they circled down. Finally, they were all perched on one long limb that extended out from the trunk of the tree and hung over the lake. There was a large hollow that could easily accommodate the seven of them for one day. But just as they were about to move into it, a young Spotted Owl appeared and hovered overhead.

"I wouldn't go in there if I were you," he said.

"Why not?" asked Gylfie.

"It's haunted."

"Haunted by what?" Otulissa asked in a testy voice as she stepped forward.

"By the scroom of a Brown Fish Owl," he said.

"Smells like fish all right." Twilight had poked his beak into the hollow.

"He was murdered," offered the Spotted Owl.

"Murdered?" they gasped.

"Yes."

"Who murdered him?" Digger asked.

"Metal Beak."

At the sound of Kludd's other name, Soren nearly toppled off the branch. If Digger hadn't quickly extended a wing to steady him, he would have. The Spotted Owl continued to hover, seeming to enjoy the fact that he had impressed these rough and wordly owls. "It was really a racdrop sort of deal."

"What do you mean?" Gylfie asked sharply.

"Well, this Brown Fish Owl tried to help Metal Beak. That owl flew in here almost burning up, feathers smoking, his mask melting, more dead than alive. The Brown Fish Owl nursed him back to health. Soon as he was well, he turned around and killed the Brown Fish Owl. How's that for gratitude? Can you believe it?"

Unfortunately they all could.

"So it's the Brown Fish Owl's scroom that haunts this place?" Otulissa asked.

"That's what they say," the Spotted Owl replied in a casual tone.

"Well, let them say," Otulissa continued. "I don't believe in scrooms. And besides, if such a scroom exists he must be a nice one, and perhaps he can nurse Soren here, who has a broken tail-feather shaft."

"Ouch! That must hurt," said the Spotted Owl.

"You're darned right it hurts," Soren said, somewhat revived from the shock of hearing his brother's name. His whole body seemed to be throbbing with the pain.

"What's your name?" Digger asked.

"Hortense," the Spotted Owl replied.

"Hortense!" Soren and Gylfie both shouted at once. Soren forgot his pain entirely.

"You can't be Hortense, that's a female name. You're a male," said Ruby.

"In the forest of Ambala, it doesn't matter if you are a female or male. It is a great honor to be named Hortense. She was a hero beyond compare. A hero is known by only one name in Ambala — Hortense."

The little Spotted Owl had settled down on the branch as he spoke. Now, perhaps moved by his own words, he felt he should try to do something heroic to live up to his name. "I know where there are some fat worms that might feel good on that broken tail-feather shaft. Would you like me to get some?"

"Oh, that would be very good of you," Gylfie said.

"I'll go with you," Digger offered. "The more worms, the better."

Haunted or not, the hollow felt good — even with the fishy smell. Soon Digger and Hortense were back with the worms. Otulissa and Gylfie arranged them as best they could at the base of Soren's tail feathers.

"I wish Mrs. Plithiver were here." Gylfie sighed. "Nestmaids are so much better at this than we are."

Although the worms relieved the pain, Soren seemed to grow feverish as the day continued. An infection had set in. When night fell, he was thrashing about and certainly not fit to fly. It would simply be too dangerous for him to journey in this condition. So they decided to stay. Toward midnight, Soren's breathing became uneven and labored. He seemed to be straining for each breath. The six owls were scared now, as scared as they had ever been. An unspoken thought swirled among them: *Is Soren dying?* This could not be happening after all they had been through. They had fought Metal Beak and the Pure Ones.

They had been to St. Aggie's and escaped. Soren himself had slashed Finny's neck wide open. No, Great Glaux, it simply could not be happening. But the sound of Soren's breathing was terrible. It seemed to shake the entire tree. They watched as his breast heaved with each breath. His eyes would blink open and closed, then blink open and look out, not recognizing anything. The owls were desperate. When Hortense came back with a new supply of worms, Twilight stepped out on the branch.

"The worms aren't working. Is there anything else we can do? Are there any nest-maid snakes around that could help us? Anybody at all?"

The owl thought for a moment. There was one place he could go, but it was scary. It was the aerie where two strange eagles lived with an even stranger owl named Mist. They were not particularly welcoming and Hortense's parents said it was best to leave them alone. A lot of crows lived up that way as well. And there was a grove of trees on the way to the aerie that was infested with flying snakes. They did not have wings or even wing flaps like certain flying squirrels, but they could sail through the air in spectacular leaps and coils, twists and turns, gliding from treetop to treetop. And they were considered terribly venomous. But there were some who said that small doses of their venom could have curative powers. Still, it was risky, for they were known to be hungry and mean. The eagles had made their peace with the flying snakes. But they were the only birds who had.

"Isn't there anything you could do to help us?" Gylfie had stepped up to Hortense. She was shaking with grief and fear. "We have to save him."

Hortense shook his head. "I . . . I . . . can't do anything." He turned away and flew off. He knew that the Barn Owl would be dead by morning.

Hortense flew around and around though the forest. For some reason, he could not face going home just yet. His parents had a new set of hatchlings who would be yipping away, demanding food and attention. He kept flying about. He wondered if one of the new hatchlings would be named Hortense. That would be hard to take. He thought again about the dying Barn Owl. He blinked his eyes open and shut.

The young Spotted Owl would never know exactly what made him do it, but suddenly he was carving a wide turn and climbing upward, higher and higher and higher. He was above the forest now and heading for the aerie on the very tallest peak of the mountain of Ambala. His gizzard quivered, and he could hardly hold his wings steady.

Suddenly, an eerie luminous green scrawl slithered out of the night. *I am not going yeep. I am not going yeep,* the Spotted Owl repeated to himself. He quickly dodged the flying snake.

Three more snakes came out of the night, but Hortense continued. Then he felt a presence flying near him. It was not a snake, but he could not quite see what it was. It seemed as if a corner of a cloud had been torn off and was drifting in a lazy way sometimes in his wake, sometimes off to one side, sometimes just ahead. But since it had arrived, there had been no more flying snakes.

As he approached the aerie, he saw the two immense eagles. He lighted down on the edge of the nest, which seemed as huge as the treetops over which he had been flying.

"What brings you here, young'un?" It was the male who spoke. There was a rumor that his mate couldn't say a word because her tongue had been ripped out in a battle.

"There's a Barn Owl down there," the Spotted Owl flicked his head in the direction of the lake. "He's with six other owls, and I think he's dying. His friends are really upset. Worms aren't working." He thought he heard a soft churring sound come from where the patch of cloud had settled. He looked in that direction, but there was nothing there now. He could have sworn it sounded like the churrs of a Spotted Owl.

"Tell me a little about this Barn Owl and his friends," the male eagle said. Hortense could tell that the female was listening intently, and in some wordless way, signals were passing between them.

"Well, they've fetched up in the hollow of that old sycamore, the haunted one."

"Ah-hem, so they say," said the male eagle. "The one where that poor owl Simon met his end. Simon, who only wanted to do good." The male eagle sighed. The Spotted Owl could have sworn he heard another sigh, like a dim whisper. It wasn't the female eagle but when he looked around, he saw not another soul.

"There's the wounded Barn Owl, his best friend, a little Elf Owl." He felt some sort of current go through the air. "Then there is a Burrowing Owl, and a big old huge Great Gray who looks really tough." The two eagles exchanged glances that seemed to say *Could it be?* Hortense continued with descriptions of the other three owls, but the eagles weren't interested.

"Fetch Slynella!" the male eagle blurted out to his mate. The female was immediately airborne, and then once more the Spotted Owl saw a wisp of fog, no bigger than an immature owl drifting beside her. *Was it a scroom?* he wondered.

No, the harder he looked, the clearer the shape became. It was a Spotted Owl, but a very pale one who flew a crooked path. This must be the one they called Mist. Finally, he could see her.

The female eagle and Mist returned with a flying snake. It was glowing like a scroll of green lightning.

"Meet Slynella," the male eagle said.

The young Spotted Owl began to quiver uncontrollably. If he had been flying instead of perched on the edge of the eagle's nest, he would have gone yeep. His wings hung at his side like two stones. The snake twisted her flat head toward him. Her glittering turquoise eyes fixed him in her gaze. A bright, forked tongue slipped out. It was the strangest tongue Hortense had ever seen. One side of the fork was a pale ivory color, the other was crimson.

"Enchanted, I am sssssure." The words slithered off the odd-colored tongue.

"Relax," the male eagle said to Hortense. "She won't hurt you."

"Relax," he says. He must be yoicks. Hortense knew that inches away from him was a creature with enough venom to wipe out an entire owl kingdom.

"Slynella will fly with us to the sycamore. With a careful application of her venom to the wound, this Barn Owl might be saved." The eagle paused. "If it isn't too late."

❧　　❧　　❧

Gylfie was weeping quietly in a corner of the hollow. The other five owls crouched in the shadows, helpless and too stunned with grief to move. Hortense did not hear any deep rasping breaths. He was sure that the Barn Owl must have died. But then he detected a faint movement in the sick owl's breast feathers. The hollow was not big enough for the eagles. The female merely stuck her head in and surveyed the situation. Then, in that soundless way she had, she communicated something to her mate.

"Get to work, Slynella, this is a fine owl," said the male eagle.

At that moment Digger, Gylfie, and Twilight blinked. These were the eagles who had saved them in the desert.

"Zan! Streak!" Gylfie gasped. "What are you doing here?" Then there was a huge flutter. The owls all pressed themselves against the sides of the hollow as Slynella, in one sinuous movement, slid in and hung herself in an S shape from a wood spur that projected directly over Soren.

"Calm yourselves. This snake is Soren's only hope. Only one side of her forked tongue bears the poison. If she mixes it with the contents of the other side, she can provide a powerful medicine for an infection."

The six owls stepped back.

The snake lowered herself until her head was directly above Soren's battered tail feather. Flicking madly, her tongue sought out the broken shaft. "Firssst I mussst pull out the shaft. No ssssense having a broken one. Then I can get to the wound with my tongue." Gylfie sank back against Twilight. The thought of that tongue probing Soren's wound made her knees weak.

In his feverish state, Soren saw something green and luminous swaying over him. Had that terrible scar of Finny's become green? Was it a green bolt of lightning now? He was fascinated. But why were all the others backing away? There was nothing to fear. Of this he was sure. His mind filled with thoughts. *Come on, pals. Nothing to fear here. Hey, Hortense! Hortense, I thought you were dead. No, not that Hortense. The real Hortense. The one Finny threw off the highest cliff in the hatchery. Hortense, how did you survive?*

Streak caught me. He flew in at the last minute.

Hortense, please don't tell me you're a scroom. I met the scrooms of my parents. It was too sad. Please, Hortense, you can't be a scroom. It's really going to frink me off if you're a scroom.

My, my, you have developed quite a coarse vocabulary since we last met.

Hortense, I'm serious. This conversation isn't just happening in my head is it — like with the scrooms?

"Definitely not!" It was Gylfie's voice piercing through the miasma of pain and fever. "I can't believe it. It *is* Hortense!"

"How many Hortenses are there around here?" Martin asked.

"Just one, the true one, the original," Streak said, poking his head into the hollow. "But now she prefers to be called Mist."

"Yes, that's true," the real Hortense said.

"What happened to that other Hortense?" Twilight asked.

"We sent him off. Brave little fellow, wasn't he? I'd say he did a fine job of living up to the name," Streak said.

"Brave fellow," said the real Hortense. "I think that's why he was able to see me even in my faded, somewhat tattered condition. But I wanted this to be a true reunion among old friends," Hortense said, looking at Digger and Gylfie, Twilight and Soren.

"Is Soren going to get better?" Gylfie asked.

"I think he'll make it," Streak said.

Soren's eyes blinked open. The cloudiness that dulled the deep black luster had cleared. "I can't believe it. Hortense, Streak, Zan — all here. All alive."

"And you!" Gylfie's voice broke. "You're alive, Soren. Alive!"

CHAPTER SIXTEEN
Let Us Fly, Mates! Let Us Fly!

Y ou see, this smith, the Rogue Smith of —" Streak had
begun to speak.

"The Rogue Smith of Silverveil," Twilight blurted out.

"We know her," Digger said.

"She's Madame Plonk's sister," Gylfie added. Madame
Plonk was the elegant singer at the Great Ga'Hoole Tree.

"Well, she came to see Zan and me. But it was really
Mist she asked for. She seems to see everything, and sometimes she dreams things that happen."

"Just sometimes," Mist added. "Remember, Soren and
Gylfie, I told you that because of the heavy deposits of
flecks that run in the streams and creeks of Ambala, owls
from that region can be both blessed and cursed."

Gylfie nodded.

"Remember I told you that my wings were small and
malformed because of the flecks, and that I had a grand-
mother who lost her wits entirely but my own father
could see through rock? Well, I cannot see through rock,

but sometimes I have dreams that seem to — how should I put it — look into the future. I can see things that sometimes happen in the future.

"Ever since that night when I saw the owl they call Metal Beak kill Simon, I have had terrible feelings. Glaux, I didn't realize it was your brother, Soren."

Soren blinked. The more he heard about the death of this good pilgrim owl named Simon, a Glauxian Brother, the worse he felt. He felt partly responsible for Simon's death. For if he had not wounded Kludd so terribly, Simon would have never crossed paths with him and tried to nurse him back to health.

Hortense continued. "I began to have dreams. And one of my dreams was of a great massing on a promontory that juts out into the Sea of Hoolemere. But it was all so vague. It was hard to understand the meaning of the dream, but then this rogue smith — never did give her name — came to us. And she was so agitated that she could barely tell her story. But it seems that she had heard on good authority that this awful group that chooses to call themselves the Pure Ones is led by your brother, and that they have been gathering Barn Owl recruits from all the owl kingdoms and forests. She said they are massing on Cape Glaux right now."

There was silence in the hollow as the owls stared at the faded and fragile Hortense.

"But Cape Glaux!" Soren finally spoke. "No owls would ever stay on Cape Glaux — not this time of year — unless . . ."

"Yes, precisely," Hortense said. "Unless they were planning an invasion of the Island of Hoole."

"We have to get back now!" Soren said.

"Soren," Gylfie pleaded. "You're not strong enough. The winterlies are beginning to blow across Hoolemere. You're now missing one whole tail feather — those don't grow back overnight. How will you rudder?"

"We must go. We must warn the great tree. I'll make it." Soren's dark gaze bore into the little Elf Owl. Gylfie knew him well enough to know he would never be swayed.

And so that night as First Black gathered in the Forest of Ambala, the seven owls made their preparations to leave. It was not an easy leave-taking, especially for Soren and Gylfie, who had never expected to see Hortense again.

"I don't know how to thank you," Soren said as they perched on the branch of the sycamore. "Streak and Zan, once more you have saved me. Hortense, that you are alive thrills Gylfie and me more than you can imagine. Your goodness and your selflessness have been a continuing inspiration for us. We would love for you to come with us to the Great Ga'Hoole Tree, for you have the most honorable of gizzards and a sublime heart. You would make a knight, a guardian most noble."

But Hortense just shook her head. "A visit someday perhaps, but my place is here in Ambala," she said.

Then Soren turned to Slynella.

"Slynella, I owe my life to you. You could have chosen not to come. You have spent your precious venom on me. I know that it weakened you. Streak and Hortense have told me that each time a flying snake spends its venom, it takes longer to replenish. That you did so willingly with no delay was a true sacrifice. How can I ever thank you?"

"Worthy. You are worthy. A friend of Sssstreak, a friend of Zzzzan, and a friend of Misssst issss mossst worthy. Ssssoren is ssuch a friend." As she spoke, Slynella writhed in and out of her S-shaped designs. She hung glowing in the First Black.

Then, as the dwenking moon climbed into the sky, the seven owls rose in the night. The Chaw of Chaws was heading home, but not before stopping on the fog-shrouded cliffs of Cape Glaux to see if what the Rogue Smith of Silverveil had reported was true.

The night was thinning as the black faded to gray. It was twixt time, that minute between the last vanishing drop of gray and the first tinge of the rose of the dawn. But today there would be no rose or pink or any of the pale seashell colors that sometimes stained the morning, for the winterlies were blowing hard. The morning was sloppy with spume and icy sheets of rain. The visibility was terrible and only an owl like Twilight, hatched on that silvery border of time between day and night, could see. He left the others and flew alone. Twilight could navigate in that dim time when the world was not quite black nor yet light, when the boundaries and the shapes of things became blurred with shadows and fog, and they almost seemed to melt away.

And now as he flew out from the sea-lashed cliffs under the cover of fog, he was seeing something that stilled his gizzard. Beneath him on Cape Glaux, spots of white were melting out of the gray fog. Hundreds upon hundreds of Barn Owls were gathered, their pale, heart-shaped faces tipped toward the sky studying the weather. They did not see Twilight, for with his plumage of silver-and-gray feathers, he blended in perfectly with the swirling fog. He plunged into a lower fog bank. Twilight strained his ears to see if he could pick up a scrap of anything they were saying, but it was useless. Still, he hovered in some dim hope. Then he detected the shapes of two Barn Owls who were apart from the rest. They were most likely keeping a watch, or perhaps they had flown out to scout the conditions at sea. Twilight flew into the thickest part of the fog and listened closely.

"We can't fly in this, Wortmore," said one of the Barn Owls.

"No. I doubt the High Tyto would want to risk it," replied the other.

"These winterlies can't keep up forever, though."

"There's bound to be a break soon. Wind should back around to north by northwest."

Dream on, fools! Twilight rejoiced silently. This was their chance. The Chaw of Chaws could fly it. And within the Chaw of Chaws was the weather chaw — Ruby, Otulissa, Soren, and Martin. Those four could fly through anything, for they had been taught by the master, Ezylryb.

Twilight returned. His report was brief. "The bad news is there are hundreds of them. Maybe even a thousand. The good news is they are scared to fly."

"Maybe a thousand, you say?" Digger's voice quavered.

"They could outnumber the owls of the great tree," Otulissa whispered. "How did they ever get that many?"

Soren regarded the chaw. They were scared. He was scared. And fear could be as awful as any disease, as terrible as the fever he had just survived. It could spread. It could rage. He must do something to stop it.

"We are the Chaw of Chaws. Do you forget that?" Soren asked. "We have already battled Metal Beak once. We have flown into the heart of tyranny in the St. Aegolius Canyons and flown out again. You heard Twilight say the Pure Ones are afraid to fly. We must not be afraid. You are noble birds. Never has it been more true that we seven, this Chaw of Chaws, are Guardians of Ga'Hoole. Our island stands in danger. We must go forth to warn and protect our island and our great tree with every bit of strength we have. We must not hesitate, for the battle will soon come to the shores of our island. So set your wings and point your beaks to slice the raging winterlies of Hoolemere. Bend your gizzards to the task. Let us fly, mates. Let us fly!"

CHAPTER SEVENTEEN
A Sodden Book

Far across the Sea of Hoolemere, on a small patch of beach shaped like a crescent, Ezylryb swept low and then lighted down on a pile of tangled seaweed. He studied the way the foam of the sea curled into swags. He squinted his eyes toward the Lobelian current. He had dropped his current markers two days before for a weather experiment over the dark stream that flowed out of the Ice Narrows. Ah, yes! He spotted one now in a tangle of seaweed. The current was moving at a swift pace, and the first of the winterlies was hovering above it.

With his odd, lurching gait, Ezylryb walked up to the bright bunch of feathers that he had dyed and tied to a bobble. But as he was about to pick up the marker, his eye caught something else. It was a sodden and warped book, the letters of the words bleeding into undecipherable clouds of ink. The old ryb's gizzard seemed to seize up and then give a mighty wrench that shook his entire body. It was the book he had given to Otulissa. Despite the blurred ink, he would recognize it anywhere. How had it come to this disastrous end?

The old owl was confused. His first instincts were to go to the parliament and report this. But then he blinked. No! Absolutely not. He would tell no one. He would let events take their course. He would be watchful and keep his own counsel. Time would reveal all. He was sure of one thing — this was not Otulissa's fault. No one revered books as much as that young Spotted Owl. He would bring the book back. He had learned the art of book repair from the Glauxian Brothers. He would dry it carefully in the heat of embers. He would oil its spine. He would care for the book as best he could. He bent over to pick up the book in his beak but, as he did so, there was a damp whispery breath halfway between a sigh and a moan and the spine of the book split. The sodden pages fell onto the beach. The surf, friskier than usual, lapped high and Ezylryb watched, stunned, as the water caught the remnants of the book and carried its pages out to sea. *I am a scientist,* he thought. *I am a rationalist, a reasoned thinker. I do not believe in omens, or superstitions. But something terrible seems to brew anon, on the cusp of these winterlies.*

And it was as if on the ruined pages of a book brutalized by the sea, a new story was being written.

I fear for Hoole, thought Ezylryb. *I fear for the great tree!*

Kludd perched high in the tallest tree on Cape Glaux. Beside him was Nyra, a female Barn Owl. She gazed at the High Tyto. Finally, he was hers. Together they would rule the kingdoms of owls — not just the southern ones, but the Northern Kingdoms as well. She had picked him out when he was just a nestling. True, she was older, but what did it matter? She was not that much older. She had been so young when she was with the old High Tyto. She had spotted Kludd on one of their recruiting missions through the Forest Kingdom of Tyto. There was a look in that nestling's eye. She knew he would be perfect. The old High Tyto couldn't last forever. There was no one else except herself who could lead. But they needed more heirs. There must always be eggs in a nest. They had to think of the future. The kingdoms should all be populated with Tytos, with Pure Ones. And it would be, as soon as they got to the Island of Hoole. For it was on that island in the great tree that Kludd and Nyra would have their first true nest — a nest with eggs! Young Pure Ones to hatch by spring! Oh, the very thought of it made her dizzy.

Kludd looked at his mate. His black eyes glittered darkly behind the mask. She knew he was anxious. "Soon, my dear, soon. These winterlies will ease off," she said to him.

But Kludd was lost in his own thoughts. Yes, there would be eggs. But before that, there would be death. The death of his brother. He and Nyra would plan it meticulously, as they had planned the murder of the former High Tyto more than a year before. How thrilling those early days had been when he had escaped his pathetic family. From the very start, from Kludd's first moments in the hollow of the old fir tree he had known that he had hatched into the wrong family. He was so different from them all. They were weak and stupid. He was strong. All they seemed to care about were the foolish old legends.

Oh, yes, his father knew a lot of history from the old owl kingdoms. He even had a great-grandfather who had fought in the Battle of Little Hoole and lost an eye. But all he talked about were the blessings of peace. He wouldn't even permit them to speak about battle claws. That, of course, was what caused the first really big fight between Kludd and his father.

It happened just before Soren hatched. Kludd had seen a Barn Owl fly by with battle claws. He would never forget the flash of those claws through the leafy green canopy of the forest in the full summer. It was dazzling. His gizzard had trembled with such excitement, he thought it might pop. For days, that was all he could talk about. He couldn't understand why his father had no interest in visiting the rogue smith who made them. Then the St. Aggie's raids began, and there were the rumors of egg snatching. Other families in Tyto began getting battle claws from the rogue smith to defend their hollows, and Kludd thought his father would get some, too. But he had still refused, and he continued to forbid talk of such things.

Then one day when both his parents were away, along with Mrs. Plithiver, some Barn Owls flew by — large, strong ones, and all with battle claws. One of the owls was Nyra. They stopped to chat. Kludd could hardly take his eyes off their shining claws. They didn't speak of long-ago legends. They spoke of parts of forests they had conquered, small rulers they had driven out — some they had killed. Nyra was the largest and most beautiful female Barn Owl that Kludd had ever seen. Her white feathers were so dense and gleaming, it was as if she held the moon in her face.

Kludd later discovered that there was a story told about Nyra. Like the ancient Nyra for whom she was named, she had hatched on the night of a lunar eclipse. According to some stories, the moon had dropped from the sky that night, and had risen in the face of a young hatchling. When an owl was hatched on the night of an eclipse, an enchantment was cast upon that creature. This charm was sometimes good and led to a greatness of spirit. But sometimes it was bad and led to pure evilness. In Nyra, the enchantment was bad. She was as evil as any owl could be. And when she had first glimpsed Kludd, she knew he would be perfect for the kingdom that she dreamed of — this kingdom of the Pure Ones that would rule the earth.

She could tell that, even as a nestling, his gizzard was full of blood and rage. She had spoken to the former High Tyto about the young Barn Owl. They had decided to wait until he learned how to fly, and then they would invite him to one of their ceremonies.

The ceremonies of the Pure Ones were somewhat different from those of other owls. Most owls marked the passage of their young from hatchlings to mature owls with ceremonies that celebrated such events as their consumption of First Fur on Meat, First Bones, and First Flight. The ceremonies of the Pure Ones were tests of fierceness and loyalty. There were even tests of rage. For the Pure Ones valued rage above all else. They equated it with courage.

For Kludd's first ceremony, he was required to kill a nest-maid snake of a neighboring owl family. His next ceremony demanded that he attack and maim an owl — not a Tyto, of course. A Northern Saw-whet had been found for this purpose. Kludd performed beyond Nyra and the High Tyto's wildest expectations and proved himself to be an efficient but brutal murderer. The last ceremony was often the hardest. One was required to sacrifice a family member. But Kludd was ready for the task. He had hated Soren from the moment his younger brother had hatched. He sensed that Soren was the preferred son. Soren was so much like his father. He loved the old legends, cared not a whit about battle claws, and was always the perfect little owlet. It drove Kludd mad. So pushing him out of the nest was a joyous task. He was sure that Soren had died. A defenseless owlet on the ground all night, unable to fly, should have made a tasty treat for a ground predator. Raccoons spent long evenings feasting on flightless owls and other hatchlings that had fallen from nests. When there was no sign of Soren in the morning, Kludd was sure the raccoons had gotten him. He never suspected St. Aggie's! And he would never forget his horror when Soren came flying to Ezylryb's rescue in the Devil's Triangle in Ambala. Soren had seemed full of a rage that almost matched his own! Kludd had never been so shocked in his life. He had never hated Soren so much. He had never *hated* so much. Not even when he had fought the previous High Tyto for the favor of Nyra and had first been maimed.

But even maimed, Kludd was beautiful to Nyra. She loved him more than his family ever had. In her eyes, he could do no wrong. Her passion for him was great. It was mighty, and it made him powerful. She sometimes spoke in the fragments of an ancient language of the owls of the Northern Kingdoms, from where she originally came. She would say to him in her lovely, lilting voice:

Erraghh tuoy bit mik in strah.
Erraghh tuoy frihl in mi murm frissah di Naftur, regno di frahmm.
Erragh tuoy bity mi plurrh di glauc.
E mi't, di tuoy.

The meaning of her passionate words were:

Your rage will be the jewel of my crown.
Your rage burns in me like the fires of the Naftur, ruler of the flames.
Your rage is my life's blood.
And mine, yours.

Whenever Kludd thought about this declaration of rage and love, he knew that there was nothing he could not conquer — not an owl, not a kingdom, not even the great tree. Soon it would be theirs. The winterlies were lessening. On the morrow, the siege would begin.

CHAPTER EIGHTEEN

The Great Tree Prepares

The Great Hollow was filled. Soren, Gylfie, Twilight, and Digger perched in the third balcony. Upon their return, they had immediately reported their findings to Boron, Barran, and Ezylryb. They also told the unexpected news of the forces that had gathered on Cape Glaux. In the tradition of owl kingdoms, a small delegation had been sent to try to make peace with these owls, but their efforts were in vain.

And now the owls of Ga'Hoole whispered in confusion as neither Boron nor Barran, but Ezylryb flew to the highest perch. The rest of the parliament perched in their usual places along with the two monarchs. Ezylryb began to speak.

"It is now tween time of this night, the twentieth night in the season that we owls of Ga'Hoole call white rain. A few hours ago, I received our monarchs' commission, along with the approval and the wish and the will of our parliament, to form a war cabinet. I must, with great dismay and loathing, announce that our attempts to make peace with these baleful and most brutal owls who call themselves the Pure Ones have all been in vain. These owls are determined to lay siege to our great tree and seize our island most dear.

"So now we are at war. We will persevere at war. We will make war to the very best of our ability. They are nothing but a seething mass of criminals. On our side there is quality and there is a cause that sparks the spirit and rouses the gizzard. For we fight for a good cause — the cause of compassion, of freedom, of the belief that no one owl is better than another due to birth, breed, or kind of feather.

"Now the mists and storms of the winterlies wrap our island. The so-called Pure Ones, although their numbers are great, fear flying in such weather. But we owls of Ga'Hoole fear no such whimsies of weather. Have we not flown through worse?"

There was a loud cheer from the weather and colliering chaws. "This is a solemn moment in our tree's history, but one supported by determination and hope. I would be foolish to say that the task ahead of us is not of a most grievous kind. There will be struggle. But let us not despair, for we are owls of valor, Guardians of Ga'Hoole — every one of us, young or old, Barn Owl or Pygmy,

Burrowing Owl or Boreal, Short-eared or Long-eared, Great Gray or Elf. It is in the very diversity of our breeds, the rainbow of our colors, the multiplicity of our shapes, that we find richness. We shall never submit to such a terrible and lamentable notion as that of owl purity or owl superiority. And in service to defeating such an evil and ruinous idea, we shall wage war against this monstrous tyranny that threatens all owl kingdoms. We shall wage war over sea and on the land with all the strength that Glaux gives us. Our aim is victory — victory at all costs, victory in spite of all terror. Victory, however long and hard the war may be. For without victory, there will be no survival for Ga'Hoole, the great tree, and all we have stood for; no survival for the best of the urges and impulses of owlkind, those impulses for life, for honor, and for freedom. Come then, let us go forward together to preserve owlkind."

The Great Ga'Hoole Tree thrummed with the hoots of the owls. Twilight, almost bursting out of his plumage, was already talking about how he hoped to get a set of the newest model of battle claws, the NASTs. NAST stood for Nickel Alloy Super-Talons. Bubo had forged a new kind of steel in his fires, which could be filed to a deadly sharpness. It was said that NASTs could split rock.

"What?" Twilight gasped. His unit leader, a Great Gray named Huckmore had just told Twilight, Soren, Gylfie, and the others that their mission was to lay air traps.

"We shall begin immediately weaving snares from the milkberry vines of the great tree. These have already been harvested with care. Since they are almost pure white, they will fade into the background of the snow-laden tree. But we all know how tangled these vines can get. So think of your task as setting a giant web," Huckmore said.

"I'm not a spider!" Twilight hissed.

"Be quiet," Soren hissed back.

"We have recruited nest-maid snakes from the weavers' guild, as well as some from the harp and lacemakers' guilds, to help us in the actual weaving."

"What?" Twilight whispered in complete dismay. "I'm not a nest-maid, either!"

"We know that." Gylfie gave him a kick. "We know you're a big tough owl. So grow up, Twilight. War is not all battle claws and tearing out gizzards."

"But weaving with nest-maids? You got to be kidding."

The nest-maid snakes in the Great Ga'Hoole Tree all belonged to different guilds depending on their individual talents. Mrs. Plithiver, Soren's old nest-maid, belonged to one of the most prestigious, the harp guild. She wove herself through the grass strings of the harp accompanying Madame Plonk, who sang the songs that marked the various events and times in the daily life of the owls in the tree.

"Work has already begun," Huckmore continued. "Upon completing the snares, we shall fly out to place them at strategic points on the island."

The snare unit, as they were called, followed Huckmore to a stand of tall, nearly branchless and leafless birch trees that were to serve as looms for the weaving of the webs. The warp, or the lengthwise vines, of the loom had already been fastened. At the ground level, a dozen or more nest-maids had begun to weave across the warp to create the weft, or the horizontal vines. Mrs. Plithiver was in charge of the nest-maid snake detail.

"Attention! Nest-maids," she called out. "Our unit commander has arrived." She coiled to attention, then waggled her head and touched it with her tail in a jaunty salute.

"At ease, Mrs. Plithiver," Huckmore said. "I see progress has been made."

"Yes, sir. We have almost two feet from the ground up already woven. Now, if the owls of your unit can commence weaving from the top down, I think we could easily have this finished before the Golden Talons rise in the night."

Since Mrs. Plithiver was blind, she had never seen the

constellation of the Golden Talons in the winter night sky. It was said, however, that nest-maid snakes had been blessed with extraordinary sensitivity. Although they could not see, they could detect minute changes ranging from alterations in atmospheric pressure to the movements of celestial bodies in the sky.

It did not take the owls long to get into the rhythm of weaving themselves in and out of the warp with the long strands of berries. In fact, Soren found the work rather enjoyable. If only he could forget for a moment or two the reason they were doing this. He certainly enjoyed working with Mrs. P. Normally, their schedules were so different; it was not often they got to see each other during the night.

"Lovely, Soren, lovely. You have the knack for this," Mrs. P. said. "Gylfie, dear, pull a little bit more on that last vine you flew into place." She paused and hung herself upside down. "I sense Dewlap approaching. Oh, dear."

Just then Soren caught a glimpse of Dewlap flying up to Huckmore, who was overseeing the work from a high limb in a nearby birch. He saw Huckmore shake his head wearily.

"What's going on?" Gylfie asked. With the tail end of a vine in her talons, she slid into flight next to Soren.

"I don't know. But ever since that thing with Otulissa and the flint mop, Dewlap gives me the creeps. It's almost time for my break," Soren said. "I'm going to fly around behind that tree and listen in."

"You think you can hear what they're saying from that distance?" Gylfie asked.

Soren gave her a withering glance.

"Oh, I forgot. Barn Owl!" Barn Owls were renowned for their remarkable hearing skills.

"I wish you would stop worrying about the vines, Dewlap," Huckmore was saying. "This is war. As Ezylryb said, sacrifices will have to be made. This is not going to damage the overall health of the tree. Yes, we are going to have to make do with fewer berries during the lean days of winter, but we have a good reserve and no one much cares for the berries of the white rain, anyway. They are awfully bitter."

"But I just don't think this is responsible. I am a caretaker of this tree. I can't stand by and see all these vines stripped from her," replied Dewlap.

"Look, Dewlap, I don't know how I can put this more plainly. It is a matter of life and death. If we are defeated by these owls, there is no more Ga'Hoole as we now know it. This tree will be inhabited by a bunch of criminal owls. You think they're going to take care of this tree? I don't think so, Dewlap."

Something stilled in Soren's gizzard. Huckmore was

right. If the Pure Ones captured Ga'Hoole, Kludd wouldn't spend a moment thinking about the health of the tree. Why didn't Dewlap realize this? This was what it meant to be a Guardian of Ga'Hoole. They needed the tree and the tree needed them, but sometimes there were sacrifices to keep things in balance and to guard those, as Ezylryb had called them, impulses for life, honor, and freedom.

At daybreak, Soren and his friends returned to their hollow. Digger was with a unit of Burrowing Owls from the tracking chaw, and they were assigned to digging cache holes for extra supplies around the island. Soren was anxious to talk to him.

"Listen, Digger — how's Dewlap been behaving in your unit?"

Digger blinked. "She isn't in my unit."

"What? I thought all of the Burrowing Owls were assigned to digging cache holes. I thought she was the leader."

"No. Sylvana is." Sylvana was the head of the tracking chaw so this made some sense, but she was much younger than Dewlap. Usually unit leaders were older owls.

"Well, what unit is she with?" Gylfie asked.

"Internal excavation, I think. They're enlarging some of the bigger storage hollows to hold more supplies if it really gets to be a siege. Speaking of which, Ruby in the hunting unit brought in a huge haul of those big shore rats. She is some hunter!"

Twilight yawned. "I wish I was in the hunting unit. This weaving is a bore."

"Don't worry, Twilight," Gylfie said. "By tomorrow afternoon it's going to get more interesting. We have to fly out with the snares and place them."

Soren was not listening. He was still preoccupied with his thoughts of Dewlap. Why hadn't the war cabinet placed her on the cache-hole mission? He yawned now, too. He was completely exhausted, and they would have to get up early tomorrow — by noon — to finish the last of the weaving and then set the snares. He was too tired to think about anything. He was almost too tired to dream.

But what if the snares don't work? was his last thought before he fell asleep.

Soren saw something very black and glistening, but it was just a speck at the center of a white forest lacy with snow. *How curious,* he thought as he flew closer. The speck swelled. Then his gizzard began to tremble as he counted eight huge legs. *It is just a spider, a mere insect. I am a powerful bird.* But the spider was changing before his eyes. The legs were coming together, congealing, turning from black to a feathery brown dappled with spots. And the face — the glinting face was sheathed in metal. And then he felt his own wings catch. He simply stopped flying. He had not gone yeep, but his wings, which were spread out on either side of him, were entangled in a crisscross of vines.

"Caught in your own trap!" It was his brother's voice.

"A bit of your own medicine, little brother?" Now it wasn't Kludd who spoke, but a beautiful owl whose face was whiter than the moon.

"Let me go! Let me go!"

"Wake up, Soren! Wake up." Digger and Twilight were both shaking him.

"Great Glaux." Soren was panting. "I had the worst dream. I dreamed I was caught in the snare."

"We're setting the snare for them, Soren," Twilight said. "Not them for us."

"I know that! But something happened and we got caught." He hesitated but Kludd's words flowed back. *Caught in your own trap*. And who was that owl with Kludd? She was quite beautiful.

Later that afternoon while they set the snares, the dream kept haunting Soren, especially the moon face of the beautiful owl. Had he just made her up in his imagination? Or was the dream like the ones Hortense sometimes had? Was he able to see into the future?

CHAPTER NINETEEN

At War

And so, Ezylryb, as I understand it, you are proposing that we launch our first air advances in a decoy movement in order to lure them into the snares," Boron said.

Soren, Gylfie, Twilight, and Digger huddled in the reverberating roots deep beneath the inner chamber of the parliament where the war cabinet held its most secret meetings. Soren realized that they had no right to be there. But they couldn't help it. They were just too curious, and Soren kept telling himself that maybe something good would come of it. Although he was not sure exactly what. Still, they pressed their ear slits closer to the roots. And Soren held his breath as he heard Ezylryb unfold the strategy for war to the other members of the war cabinet that included Bubo, Strix Struma, Boron, Barran, and Elvanryb, who led the colliering chaw along with Ezylryb.

"It is my suggestion that we launch this as a light-armored air division. None of our fanciest battle claws, not the NAST — at least not yet." Soren felt a tremor of excitement pass through Twilight at the very mention of the word NAST. "Let them think we're just a rag-tag outfit. There is no one better at playing decoy than Strix Struma," said Ezylryb.

"The Strix Struma Strikers shall be ready, Commander," said Strix Struma.

The four looked at one another in amazement. "She's so old!" Gylfie beaked the words silently. Strix Struma was almost as old as Ezylryb, or at least it seemed that way to the four young owls. It had been years since she had flown in battle. She had had a distinguished career and had been awarded the Ga'Hoolian Guardian Medal of Outrageous Bravery for her action at the Battle of Little Hoole. At that time, acting as windward flanking subcommander, and with no concern for her own personal safety, she had flown straight into a wedge of the advancing enemy unit, fracturing their formation and thus shattering their forces. But that had been years ago, long before any of them — or even their parents — had hatched.

Bubo then gave a report on the coals he had buried with special insulation to keep them hot, so that they could fight with fire when necessary. The four owls felt very proud when it was mentioned how successful the Chaw of Chaws had been in both the use of fire and the rescue of Ezylryb, months before. Ruby, in particular, was mentioned. So it seemed as if the four of them and Ruby, Martin, and Otulissa might be called upon in any fire-fights. The rest of the meeting was rather dull, mostly talk about supplies and cache holes.

The four owls were careful to leave the roots sepa-rately and take different paths back to their hollow. They had vowed not to talk about anything they had heard ex-cept in the privacy of their hollow, for one never knew who might be listening. Now all they had to do was wait for their orders, and for the Pure Ones. But Soren had to admit that there was comfort in knowing that some were not simply waiting. Strix Struma would be flying out just after First Black with her light-armored division, the Strix Struma Strikers, to engage the enemy.

"I wonder who is in the Striker division," Gylfie said.

"It's top secret," Twilight replied. "Probably only the most experienced warriors."

"Great Glaux, I hope they aren't all as old as Strix Struma," Digger said.

In another hollow, Otulissa was waiting, too. She waited and trembled. Her gizzard had not stopped flinch-ing all day, ever since the afternoon when she had been awakened and told that they would fly tonight. Now she was scared to death. How had it all changed so quickly?

When she was told that she had been selected for the elite and secret Striker force, she had been so excited. Her main worry was that she would accidentally tell her friends — especially Twilight. Glaux, Twilight would be so jealous. And to be chosen for her hero's special force! She had never imagined anything so sublime. For Otulissa had always worshipped Strix Struma. Strix Struma was her model for everything — manners, brains, elegance, gizzardly instincts. But now it was war, and all those proud feelings seemed to vanish. She could die within a few hours. It had been different in that battle in the forest when they had rescued Ezylryb. There were fewer owls to fight, and it had all happened so quickly. There wasn't time to get nervous.

There was no sense in trying to sleep for the rest of the day. She would have to get up in a few hours, anyway. Besides, Otulissa wasn't worried about being tired. It was hard to be tired when one was so scared. Her gizzard was twitching as if it were having its own private electrical storm. Her first stomach was tight as a drum — she couldn't imagine eating anything. Her brain was buzzing with all those equations they had learned about wind drift, flying with claws, and how to calculate drag and lift. Glaux, she was scared. Her eyes filled with tears as she thought of never seeing her friends again.

Soon another Spotted Owl stuck his head into Otulissa's hollow and nodded to her. *Well, this is it,* she thought. *This is war.*

The island had been divided into quadrants. And each of the four quadrants had then been divided into four other sections. The heaviest defenses were in the southwestern quadrant, as this was the most sensible angle of attack for an enemy — especially an enemy that did not like flying in adverse weather conditions. The prevailing north to northwest wind would give them an advantage, allowing them to fly in on a quartering tailwind as opposed to flying directly against a headwind. This would give them a bit of a boost. The Strix Struma Strikers would not have this advantage, for they would have to fly against this wind, not head-on but enough to slow their flight. This did not disturb Strix Struma. The Guardians, particularly the Strike force, were masters of slow flight. In the turbulent air over the Sea of Hoolemere, this was important.

Soren, Gylfie, and Twilight took up their positions on top of two snares in a section of the southwestern quadrant. It was a perfect vantage point. They watched in stunned amazement as the Striker force flew out into the spume-laced air with Otulissa flying in a flanking position and Ruby ahead of her. Ruby, they understood. Ruby was one of the most superb fliers of the tree, but Otulissa?

"It must have killed her to keep quiet about this," Gylfie offered as they watched the Striker force dissolve into a fog bank.

"Let's just hope she doesn't get killed," Soren said.

"She won't. She'll do fine." Soren and Gylfie swung their heads toward Twilight, and blinked in surprise. This was not the reaction they had expected. They had thought that Twilight, of all owls, would be insanely jealous of Otulissa's being chosen for this mission. "She's smart, and you know how sensitive all Spotted Owls are to pressure changes — almost as good as nest-maid snakes. And she'll be brave — if only for Strix Struma, she'll show courage. If she can just stop yakking and keep her beak shut, she'll do fine."

At that moment, Huckmore came up to them. "Now you understand what to do when the enemy is driven into the snares by the Striker force. You are to pull the slipknot lines, which will immediately immobilize the enemy. Many will die instantly. If they are caught around the neck, this can result in strangulation. If their wings are ensnared, they are usually broken. Any questions?"

Soren, Gylfie, Twilight, and three other owls working this snare all shook their heads.

"Good luck, Guardians!" Soren felt a little thrill course through his gizzard. This was the first time any of them had ever been addressed by an elder member of the tree as Guardians. None of them had had their Guardian ceremony yet, but this old Great Gray who had seen many battles himself had called them Guardians!

There was no need to tell them to keep a sharp eye out for incoming owls. They could hardly take their eyes off the action that was just commencing off the shores of the island. A flying wedge of Sooty Owls was approaching fast. Behind them were at least forty owls — some Sooty, a few Grass Owls, and many Barn Owls, their faces fading into the tossed-up spray of the breaking waves. Just as they passed over the beach, they unlocked their claws. The Strikers materialized, seemingly coming out of nowhere. They had split their force into two divisions. At twenty owls they were half the number of the enemy, but they struck the center of the wedge from two sides, thus shattering the formations. The point of the wedge remained intact but with only ten determined owls to stay their course toward the island's center and the tree. Still, it was a brilliant maneuver. Now ten enemy owls advanced. They were maddened that their force had been shattered, but were more resolute than ever in their quest. Yet through their rage, they were not quite so alert. In the foggy night of the snow-laden forest, they were not able to distinguish the white vines from the trees.

"Voles dance at dawn!" Huckmore's lieutenant called out the code to prepare to tighten the slipknots. Soren and Gylfie were at their stations. They wore no battle claws because it was too hard to work the vines with claws on.

"Steady. Steady. Steady," Gylfie whispered. It was important that they didn't panic, that they pull the slipknots at precisely the right moment — not too soon, not too late.

Soren could feel the wind generated by the flapping owls. "LOVELY." The word sailed out into the night, a strange word in battle, but the essence of code was to deceive the enemy and communicate with the allies. So instead of "Now!" or "Strike!" the gentle, two-syllable word had been chosen as the call to action for the snare rippers, as Soren, Gylfie, and the others who minded the vines were called.

The impact of the in-flying owls sent tremors through the web. Soren saw tiny Gylfie yanked up and down, but she held tight to the vine. Horrible screeches raked the air as the enemy owls, in a panic, tried to extricate themselves. Ten owls hung, some already lifeless, others broken and dying in the snare.

The first battle had been won. Scattered enemy owls had been snagged in the deadly snares.

But on the far side of Hoolemere, where the wind swept down like sharp blades from the Ice Narrows, a small division of owls led by Nyra and Kludd pressed against the fierce headwinds. Kludd looked at his mate with admiration. As a native of the Northern Kingdoms, she knew these winds. She knew the vagaries of their sudden switches that created stormy eddies and whirlpools of air. And she knew, as she had told Kludd, that this side of Hoolemere would be lightly defended and easily penetrated.

Just wait until the hireclaws arrive. Her gizzard stirred with excitement at the thought, and she turned to Kludd. "We may have lost the first battle, my dear. But we shall win the war!"

CHAPTER TWENTY
The News Is Not Good

The wind had died and the snare waved languidly in the occasional remnant gusts. Soren scanned the vines. One severely wounded owl had been extricated and flown off in an airborne hammock between two Boreal Owls who worked as matrons in the infirmary. It was odd. Soren thought that the very vines that had caused injury and death could also be woven to make rescue transports. Nine owls hung in macabre configurations of death with their wings twisted and their heads askew. There was nothing particularly glorious or heroic about war, Soren realized. It was really nothing more than a grubby, vile task to vanquish a foul tyranny led by his own brother. Even Twilight seemed subdued in the face of the sheer ugliness that had now been woven into the snare. It seemed so strange to Soren that the same motions that wove beautiful music from the harp of Madame Plonk or the beautiful tapestries and laces that hung in the Great Ga'Hoole Tree had now been used to weave this cloth of death. He could not wait to leave the snare. The relief snare rippers were expected soon. Soren was completely exhausted.

Back in the tree there were no victory speeches or celebrations over the repulsion of this first attack. Instead there was an uneasy quiet that seemed to flow through the tangle of corridors in the tree. The enemy's forces had been decimated, but they were said to have thousands, and there were rumors of hireclaws, rogue owls belonging to no kingdom, who could be hired to go into battle for the price of a good set of battle claws.

"Where's Otulissa?" Gylfie said. "She must be back."

"Up in the infirmary," Digger said as he dropped onto a pile of down and stuck his legs straight out in the peculiar posture that he used for sleeping.

"The infirmary!" they all exclaimed.

"Don't worry. It's just a scratch. She didn't even want to go, but they made her," he said.

"We should go visit her," Soren said. "But I'm just too tired."

"We can all go later," Digger replied.

They were all so exhausted that they thought they would fall asleep immediately. But they didn't. Perhaps it was the unease that seemed to pervade the great tree.

"They must know about the snares now," Twilight mused out loud.

"They'll be more careful next time, won't they?" Soren said.

"You can't keep something like that a secret forever," Gylfie said.

"I heard that the secret was already out in some parts of the western quadrant," Digger said.

"What?" Gylfie asked.

"Yes, and Sylvana is worried that some of those caches we've buried have already been disturbed."

"Which ones?" Twilight asked.

"The ones with the coals," he replied.

"Our firepower?" Twilight had lofted to his perch in great alarm. "That's us!" Twilight meant the Chaw of Chaws. They had been recruited for the Flame Squadron, or as they were sometimes called, the Bonk Brigade. Bonk flames were blue with a flicker of yellow in the center and a tinge of green at the edges. They were intensely hot. These were the same flames that made the fires in Bubo's forge full of bonk, the best fires for forging metals.

All this news was very disturbing. But finally the owls fell asleep.

"You can go in only if you promise to be very quiet," the burly Short-eared matron said as she led Soren, Gylfie, Twilight, and Digger into the infirmary which she supervised. "And no talking to that Barn Owl, she's an official prisoner of war."

Soren, Digger, Gylfie, and Twilight exchanged glances.

That must be the one who got caught in our snare, Soren thought.

Otulissa was tucked into a downy croft, as they called the beds of the infirmary. She looked perfectly fine to Soren.

"You don't look hurt at all," Gylfie said.

"I'm not!" Otulissa snapped. "It's simply ridiculous that I'm being kept in here."

"What happened?" Soren asked.

"I took a very light hit on my port side. They insisted I come here for observation because Strix Struma thought I was flying funny."

"Funny?" Gylfie asked.

"Out of balance, that's all. I'm flying fine now. I straightened out on the way back. I think they are being awfully cautious."

"What was it like?" Twilight said. "Out there you flew straight into the first wedge of the enemy. How did you do it?"

Otulissa twisted her head almost entirely around to indicate the Barn Owl in the other croft. "Supposedly she's unconscious, but you never can tell. So I can't talk about anything having to do with the war. Nor should you."

"Oh," Twilight said.

"What else is there to talk about?" Digger offered.

It was true, of course. Soren was observing Otulissa. She seemed different somehow. Maybe this was what flying straight against the enemy did to an owl.

At just that moment, Dewlap stuck her head into the infirmary hollow. "Oh, great Glaux, Otulissa, what are you doing here?" She seemed stunned to find the Spotted Owl in the infirmary.

"She's been hurt," Gylfie said. "That's why she's here."

Stupid old owl! Soren thought. *Why else would she be here?*

"Why are you here, Dewlap?" Digger asked.

"Well, I'm . . . I'm . . ." she began to stammer, then snapped, "I am here visiting the wounded."

Otulissa swung her head directly at the Ga'Hoolology ryb. Her amber gaze bore into Dewlap. "That's so kind of you to come, even if you didn't know I was here. Thank you very much. I'm sure the others wounded will be touched by your gesture."

Dewlap seemed to have recovered her poise. "Yes. I, of course, wasn't sure who would be here, but I felt a visit was one very small kindness I could bestow in these troubled times." And then she seemed distracted and her eyes grew misty and seemed to focus on something very far away. "Who would have ever thought it would all come to this?" she said softly, more to herself than anyone else. "To war," she said in a low whisper.

Soren, Twilight, and Gylfie spent two more nights on the snares but they caught very few owls. There was, in fact, very little action. Again, there was a disturbing silence. The winterlies had abated, although the temperatures had dropped dramatically. Ice floes were beginning to form in the Sea of Hoolemere. Rations were running short, for food had to be conserved. And although hunting units went out, it was so cold it seemed as if all the prey had taken to their burrows and were locked beneath the frozen earth. The nights were long and black, as the moon had dwenked and would not be back for several days.

One night just before dawn as Soren, Gylfie, and Twilight finished snare detail, they sensed that something had changed within the tree. There was an anxious buzz but they could catch only fragments of hasty exchanges. Every time they passed one of the older owls, beaks seemed to clamp shut.

"I heard something about a skirmish on the far side of the island," Digger said, slipping into his place at Mrs.

Plithiver's table. She had stretched her body to its maximum length so more of the owls could be accommodated. Primrose, Eglantine, and Martin crowded around the rosy-scaled table that Mrs. P. provided with her wonderfully pliant body. Ga'Hoole nut cups filled with watered-down milkberry tea were placed next to minced mouse. It was not the fare they were accustomed to, but no one dared complain. A month from now they might be looking back on this as a magnificent repast. The winters on the Island of Hoole were normally long and harsh, and now with war, even harsher.

"Attention!" It was the booming voice of Boron. "Ezylryb, our minister of war, has requested to address us at this breaklight meal."

Ezylryb, looking quite haggard, flew to the top perch in the dining hall. "I shall be direct and concise. I am afraid the news is not good. Many days have passed since this war began. We have met with great successes on the western front. But on the northeastern shores, in a quadrant where we thought ourselves invulnerable because of the fierceness of the winter seas combined with the wrathful winds out of the Ice Narrows, we have sustained harsh losses in an unexpected enemy attack. You have heard rumors of a skirmish. I fear it was more than that. A substantial number of enemy troops have broken through our defenses.

While our own troops were diverted by this action in the northeastern quadrant, other forces attacked in the southwest. An invading force has landed and more may come. What we have thus far called the Battle of the Coasts is over, and I expect that the Battle of Hoole is about to begin. Our civilization of owlkind depends upon this battle, as the whole fury of these base and most ignoble owls who call themselves the Pure Ones is turned upon us.

"But we must not fear. We have on this island today some of the finest fighters in owlkind. We have our Strix Struma Strikers, our Flame Squadron, our squadrons of Burrowing Owls who, with their long legs and talons sublime, can dig like the best of any burrowing animal on earth. And they can fight, too, I might add! With these fine owls, we shall defend our island. You shall not, however, be called upon immediately for offensive action. First, we shall try a defensive strategy. We shall not be very mobile, but we will be strong. We shall fortify ourselves within the massive trunk of this, our great tree, so lovingly cared for through the centuries. It continues to be cared for under the guidance of our invaluable ryb of Ga'Hoolology, Dewlap."

Ezylryb nodded to the Burrowing Owl, and she lowered her head shyly. Soren felt Otulissa, who had been released from the infirmary, grow smaller. In truth, she had not diminished, but her fear had grown huge. It rattled through her hollow bones.

What is going on here? Soren wondered. He listened as Ezylryb continued to explain the defensive strategy. "We have enough food to hold out, more than they will have in these coming months. Yes, there will be rough times ahead, but we can bear the discomfort with patience and with fortitude. We shall never surrender to these false ideals, to these twisted notions of superiority, to this tyranny of purity."

Otulissa looked at Soren. "I can't stand it!" she whispered.

"Can't stand what?" Soren asked.

"How Ezylryb was going on about Dewlap. Look at her gloating up there."

"Let her gloat, Otulissa," Digger said.

"What do you mean?" Soren asked. Otulissa looked equally surprised by Digger's remark.

"Think about this: Dewlap is the only Burrowing Owl who has not been put on a digging unit. We are all burrowing something. I'm doing cache holes for embers. Hubert over there is caching food supplies. Muriel and three others are excavating the existing storage areas under the tree to make them larger. If Ezylryb thinks Dewlap is so great, why isn't she working in a unit?" Digger asked.

"Isn't she supervising?" Soren asked.

"Not really," Digger says. "Supposedly she is overseeing the storage area excavations under the tree, but it's sort of a fake job. We all know how to do it. She just arranges the shifts we dig in and keeps the inventory lists. So don't get that upset, Otulissa. I don't think Ezylryb is sincerely 'going on about Dewlap.'"

"Then what's he doing?" Soren asked.

"Now that's the real question," Digger said. "And I can't answer it." He paused. "Yet."

There was no doubt in Soren's mind that, of himself, Digger, Twilight, and Gylfie, Digger was the deepest thinker and the most reflective. Gylfie might be considered the smartest because she was a quick learner, and she knew a lot. Twilight was too impulsive to be considered a deep thinker, although he was brilliant at perceiving small gradations of light as night shifted to day and day to night. And Soren himself — well, Soren wasn't really sure how he would describe his own mental activities. But Digger made connections that others might not ever think about. And the connections he was making now both fascinated and alarmed Soren.

CHAPTER TWENTY-ONE

Besieged

The great old tree creaked in the winter gales that lashed the island. Bitter cold air niggled through the cracks and crevices. In Soren's hollow, they hung the furry hide of a possum that Twilight had once killed to block the drafts. It did block the draft, but none of them could quite believe they had ever feasted on possum. There was no fresh meat left, only cured, dried meat that was bloodless and about as tasty to eat as tree bark. It was rumored that even the Ga'Hoole nuts were running low. Soren and his friends had all grown thinner. There was no doubt about it. Their feathers were less lustrous, their eyes somewhat dimmer. When the portions in the dining hollow had first started to dwindle, they would recall past meals they had eaten.

"Oh, remember the milkberry tart, the one Cook made with the maple syrup?" someone would say.

"I'd settle for just the maple syrup," someone else would say. And so it would go. But now no one talked about such things. They were still hungry — hungrier than ever — but they had somehow grown used to the gnawing in their stomachs. To wish for a milkberry tart seemed frivolous. They now only wished to live and not starve to death.

And when the backbone of winter broke, as it would in a few weeks, when the ground began to thaw and the owls' prey began to emerge from their burrows and holes, would they even be able to hunt? The enemy was out with their reinforcements of hireclaws, and they had encircled the great tree. They would be the first to pounce on the emerging prey. They were tightening the noose around the tree to cause starvation. If the Guardians could not fly over their usual hunting grounds, they would surely starve and the enemy would grow fat.

"What are you doing, Soren?" Twilight asked. "Hoping for a bug to eat?" Soren had been scratching in the dirt beneath the perches of their hollow. He had felt too weak to even loft himself to his usual perch, which was much better for holding conversations than staying on the floor. But no one talked much these days. He had begun by scratching idly with his talon. But a design seemed to emerge.

"What is that?" Gylfie said, coming over to look.

Soren blinked. "It's us."

"What do you mean?" she asked.

"You see, here's the tree and we are all in the tree, and here is the enemy, all around us. They can't get in, because we don't have any weak points in the tree, but we can't get out. As Ezylryb said, this defensive strategy isn't very mobile."

"In other words, we're stuck," Twilight said. "So what else is new?"

"But what if we could get out?" Soren asked. Soren felt Digger stir beside him.

"Digger," said Soren. " What if we could dig out? Could we burrow out with our forces and then deploy our troops to two points, and catch them between us?" Soren lifted his foot in the air and snapped his two front talons together in the same quick movement used to catch bats on the wing. Their gizzards all began to twitch with nervous excitement. Then Gylfie said the word, the name that made it all seem possible.

"Octavia!"

"A pincer movement! Of course, I think it might be possible," the old snake who tended the nests of both Madame Plonk and Ezylryb spoke in her slow ponderous manner with the inflections of the Northern Kingdoms. Octavia, unlike the other snakes who all had rosy to pale pink scales, had a greenish-blue hue. She was a Kielian snake from Stormfast Island in the Bay of Kiel. Kielian snakes were known for their incredible musculature. They could actually dig holes.

It was Ezylryb who had seen how useful these snakes, who were not blind like the rosy-scaled nest-maid snakes, could be in battle. He had come up with the idea for a stealth force of Kielian snakes that could tunnel into enemy territory. This was during a period when the War of the Ice Claws was raging in the Northern Kingdoms. On one of her missions in the stealth force, Octavia was blinded and Ezylryb lost not only his mate, but one talon. Ezylryb and Octavia, both maimed by war, had withdrawn from the military life and sought refuge for many years on an island in the Bitter Sea where the Glauxian Brothers had a retreat. Now, however, it was war again.

"Would Ezylryb think this could work?" Soren asked tentatively.

"You'll never know until you ask him. I could be of help in the tunneling, even though I'm not quite as fit as I used to be," said Octavia.

"Well, there are all the digging units, the Burrowing Owls," Digger said excitedly.

"Yes, yes," Octavia said slowly. But she seemed to hesitate as if there were something more she wanted to say.

"Should we go to Ezylryb now and ask him? Should we ask the parliament?" Digger asked.

"No!" Octavia spoke abruptly, then coiled up and swung her head. "Now listen carefully. Say nothing of this to anybody, not even Otulissa or Martin or any of your other Chaw of Chaw mates. I'm glad you found me in the corridor and asked me to your hollow. I think Ezylryb should come here as well to listen to this plan. I don't know how to say this exactly, but there have been certain breeches in security. There have been information leaks. It is suspected that the parliament hollow is not completely secure."

Soren and the three others tried not to gasp. They were the only ones who knew about the strange phenomenon that allowed the roots to transmit sound beneath the parliament chamber, or at least they thought they were. Had they been discovered? Had their listening post been discovered?

"Wait here," Octavia said. "I'll be back with Ezylryb soon. There's not a minute to waste." And the old Kielian snake slithered out of their hollow, her green scales glowing in the dim light.

CHAPTER TWENTY-TWO
Coo-Coo-Coo-Roo

Ezylryb looked down at the scratchings Soren had made in the dirt. His bad eye seemed to grow squintier as he studied the small Xs that Soren had drawn, which stood for the Guardian troops.

"It's going to take time, almost a month, I should think," Ezylryb said.

"A month!" Digger gasped. "Sir, there are three units of Burrowing Owls. We could do it in less than a week."

"Well, you see, that is the problem. This must remain absolutely top secret. The fewer owls who work on it, the better. This place is leakier than a rotted-out stump." Octavia nodded in agreement. "I want only three owls working on it from the Burrowing units — you, Digger, Sylvana, and Muriel."

"Not Dewlap?" Soren said.

"Not Dewlap." There was an uncomfortable silence and then Octavia coughed slightly.

"Lyze," she said. Only Octavia ever called Ezylryb Lyze,

his old name from the Northern Kingdoms, and she rarely used the name in front of other owls. "If I may suggest something."

"Of course, my dear." Ezylryb's usually gruff voice always softened when the old Kielian spoke to him.

"Why couldn't Twilight, Soren, and Gylfie help out on this project? They aren't Burrowing Owls, but why should they stand by idly? I am sure under the guidance of Digger, they could become adequate excavators. With their help, the work might go a little faster."

"That is an excellent idea, Octavia." He swiveled his head toward the other three owls. "Well, young'uns, what do you say? Think you can learn the ways of the Burrowers?"

"Yes, sir!" the three owls responded at once.

"Then I think you must begin immediately."

It was hard work. It was dirty work. But even though they were not the robust owls they once had been because of the short food rations, the six owls found a new energy. The cause itself seemed to feed them, for they were digging their way to freedom. Octavia helped out as well. Despite her age and her girth, she proved particularly nimble at tunneling out some of the trickier turns.

Soren would have never guessed it, but Burrowing Owls were a talkative lot when they worked. They had songs they sang to set the rhythm for the digging, and they had loads of stories of the great legends of the Burrowing Owl world. There was one Burrowing Owl, a female known as Terra, who was renowned for having, in just one night, dug a burrow that tunneled straight through a mountain.

Sylvana herself could have been a legend, Soren thought. She was an exceptionally pretty owl, and Soren marveled at how featherless legs, which he used to think of as rather revolting, could suddenly seem so lovely to him. White and exceedingly thin but muscular, Sylvana's legs flashed in the faint light of the tunnel like lightning crackling in the summer sky as she dug furiously. Sylvana had started to sing a digging song that had quickly become Soren's favorite. The *coo-coo* call was the call of the Burrowing Owl, and their voices were lovely and almost dovelike as they all joined in song. Soren felt rather shrill by comparison whenever he tried to use the call that wove through the song, but Sylvana never criticized him. She encouraged everyone.

> *Coo-coo-coo-ROOOO!*
> *Coo-coo-coo-ROOOO!*
> *Burrow, scrape,*
> *Excavate*
> *Through gravel, ice, hard-packed earth*

Through sand, through muck, through mire.
We pit, we dig, we gouge,
and never do we tire.
Our legs are bare,
Our talons sharp,
We drill the earth and know the spots
Where rock crumbles into soil,
Where shale can shift and slide like oil.

Coo-coo-coo-ROOOO!
Coo-coo-coo-ROOOO!

We shall burrow through and through.

When they returned to their hollow from their work, they would fall into an exhausted sleep. But the work was good. They were making progress. When Octavia could, she would sneak them extra food rations as Ezylryb had asked her to do. But she had to be careful so as not to arouse suspicion.

The plan was to excavate a tunnel that extended to an old fir tree that had been blown down in the winterlies. It was a rotten old tree and the stump was nearly hollow, which would provide them with an easy way out and into a flight zone that was well beyond the position of the enemy. Once the tunnel was completed, not only would the Strix Struma Strikers be able to get out, but the other tactical units would as well. These divisions would then encircle the enemy and begin a pincer movement. The besiegers would become the besieged.

Now, after only two weeks of hard work, they were almost there. Sylvana estimated that there were only another four days of work, five at the most.

"You should be proud," she said at the end of their shift. "You especially, Soren, Twilight, and Gylfie. This did not come naturally to you." Muriel and Digger nodded. "But you have learned to excavate as finely as any Burrowing Owl."

At just that moment, Octavia slithered down the tunnel. "I'm sorry to interrupt, but Sylvana, there is a problem."

"What's the problem?" Sylvana asked.

"Dewlap."

"Dewlap?"

Soren felt a queasiness in his gizzard, and he looked at Digger.

"I'm not sure what it's all about, Sylvana, but Ezylryb wants to see you at once in his hollow."

"Well, I'll be right there."

"A special project? That sounds interesting. You know, Ezylryb, I never complain. But I just feel that I am being left out. I am not being given the respect a ryb deserves," Dewlap said.

Ezylryb sighed. *This is going to be tricky,* he thought. *How can I be sure she is the one responsible for the leaks? To call an owl a spy is a terrible thing. But we have to find out. There is no choice.*

If Dewlap had been a spy, Ezylryb also wondered if it was entirely her fault. Could the Pure Ones have appealed to her sense of duty about the care and maintenance of the tree? Dewlap was a fanatic about the health of the Great Ga'Hoole Tree. It was the great tree at all costs, even if those costs might be in the form of lives of the owls for whom the tree was home.

"My dear, you must understand that I am only trying to conserve your strength as I have with Strix Struma, Elvan, and other rybs during this siege. We are so much older than the young'uns and on short rations, we simply do not have the energy they have. But with this special project, I feel that you are the only one who could do it," Ezylryb said.

This was proving more difficult than Ezylryb had anticipated, but he suddenly had the idea of the special project, and that was why he had sent for Sylvana. Now he only could hope that Sylvana would be the quick study he believed her to be, for there was really no time to explain.

"Ah, Sylvana, here you are. Now let me explain why I called you. You see, Dewlap feels that she could serve more and do much more than she is now doing in this siege. And for some time I have been turning over in my mind a project that I now think is perfect for Dewlap. It could, Glaux bless us, even get us out of this terrible siege situation."

Sylvana blinked. *What is he talking about?* she wondered.

Ezylryb continued. "You see, I am imagining a tunnel that burrows out of the south root lines of the tree toward the point where the sea funnels in beneath the cliffs. I have done the geodetic studies of that region of the island, and I realize that if we could excavate a tunnel to that point, there is a natural earth vent there through which we could exit."

Brilliant! Sylvana thought. Dewlap would be working on a tunnel in the *opposite* direction of their own tunnel. It would get Dewlap out of Sylvana's feathers. Dewlap had always been jealous of Sylvana, perhaps because of her youth, perhaps her beauty, or perhaps her skills. Not only was Sylvana a remarkable excavator, but considering she was a Burrowing Owl (whose flight skills were usually considered inferior), Sylvana was a skillful and elegant flier. Her wing work was a thing of beauty.

"Well, what about you joining me in this tunnel project, dear?" Dewlap asked and cocked her head toward Sylvana in that insufferable way she had. Sylvana blinked. What could she say? If she said she was too busy, Dewlap would want to know with what. If she just said no, she would merely sound disagreeable. She looked at Ezylryb. He gave her an almost imperceptible nod.

"Yes, of course." Sylvana bowed her head slightly. "It would be an honor to serve with you in our battle against these tyrants."

Dewlap seemed a bit flustered. Perhaps she had not expected capitulation so quickly from the young and beautiful ryb. "Yes, yes," she twittered nervously, and she said once more what she had said in the infirmary when she had poked her head in and seen Otulissa, "Who would have ever thought it would all come to this? To war?"

What a strange thing to say, Sylvana thought. She blinked just as Soren had when Dewlap had said the same thing to him.

CHAPTER TWENTY-THREE
The Last Battle

Through code, each of the main tactical units had been alerted only minutes before the tunnel was completed to report to a region deep within the roots of the tree. It was an odd place to meet. The usual area for mission briefings was in a space off the dining hollow. But now as the night began to fall, scores of owls squashed into a very small chamber that appeared to have been freshly excavated. A makeshift perch had been created for Ezylryb to address the troops. As his gaze swept over the owls, he could see confusion in their eyes.

"For the last several weeks a small unit of Burrowing Owls aided by three non-Burrowers has been engaged in a most secret mission. With an industry that can only be called extraordinary, considering the deprivations we have all endured, these owls have created a tunnel leading out of the great tree to a point beyond the enemy lines."

There was a gasp of amazement from the gathered owls.

"Chart, please!" Ezylryb swiveled his head toward Octavia, who unfurled a hide chart on which he had marked the positions of the enemy troops in relation to the great tree.

"A small reconnaissance unit led by Octavia managed to slip out through a very small opening before the tunnel was entirely finished. They reported back to us that the majority of the enemy troops have gathered at a region directly opposite the termination of our tunnel. In other words, they are here." He indicated with his mangled talons the south root lines of the tree. "The enemy seems to be regrouping there. This works in our favor."

Ezylryb then went on to explain the pincer movement that would be put into operation. There was complete silence. One could have heard a feather drop, but at the same time there was almost an electrical buzz as gizzards churned with excitement. All the owls would be called upon to rise into this darkness with their units. Twilight, Soren, and the rest of the Chaw of Chaws would be flying with the Flame Squadron. They would hold burning branches that had been ignited in the caches of buried coals. Barran's Elite Talons and the Elvan Flying Screechers would fly with new NAST battle claws. Ruby and Otulissa would be flying with fire in the Strix Struma Strikers unit.

"We shall strike out in a classic pincer movement. We

have the advantage of the wind at our backs. And the latest reports are that the wind has shifted even more in our favor. The majority of the enemy troops are trapped in an unworkable airspace. We all are trained in flying low just above the turbulent crashing waves of the Sea of Hoolemere. We shall try to draw them down for close sea flight, and many of them will drown." Ezylryb could feel the growing confidence of the troops. "My trust in your abilities to fight this battle to the finish — to a victorious and glorious finish — does not waver, but grows by the second. We are few compared to these evil owls, but as I have said before, numbers are not everything. And never in the history of conflicts of owlkind has so much been owed to so few. And now I say, go forth. Go forth for our island, go forth for our tree, go forth for honor and all that we imagine when we think of the civilization wrought by our Guardians of Ga'Hoole. Once more I say, be ye owls of valor. Glaux Bless."

The owls began to stream into the entrance to the tunnel. Within minutes they would be out for the first time in so long, out into the air, out in flight. The Flame Squadron, or Bonk Brigade, knew upon exiting exactly which coal caches they must go to. With so many blowdowns from the winter storms, finding branches to ignite would be easy.

The night air felt wonderful as it struck Soren's face. And, oh, to fly again! Within seconds, the squadron had their branches ignited.

Except for Ruby and Otulissa, who with their flaming branches flew flanking positions in the Strix Struma Strikers, the Chaw of Chaws rose in the air. Martin flew beside Soren. Twilight flew point. Thick fog had pushed in, making their flaming branches less visible. The flames looked like dim smears of light in the sky.

The enemy did not see them until it was too late. There was a shrill alarm hoot, but the Bonk Brigade was suddenly upon them. Sweeping widely with his branch, Soren knocked out two large Barn Owls. They tumbled toward the sea with feathers singed. They tried to climb out of the turbulent air that was kicked up by the crashing waves, but every time they came up, the Strix Struma Strikers would force them back down. Ezylryb was right. These owls could not fly low in these conditions. Soren scanned the night for his brother. He hoped that he would not have to encounter him again. "Port side, Soren!" someone cried out.

An owl with a huge luminous face was flying directly toward him. A streak of blood coursed diagonally across her face. It was as if the moon had been slashed and was bleeding. Her battle claws were extended and gleamed through the fog. Soren's branch had caught some seawater and had begun to fizzle miserably. There was no time to get back to a coal cache for a reignition. Great Glaux, he was virtually defenseless, for the Flame Squadron wore only the lightest of battle claws. They were nothing compared to what this owl was wearing.

Martin, flying nearby, quickly assessed the situation. "Soren, we'll lead her on a merry." A "merry" was code for the low layers of turbulent air just above the water which the Guardians of Ga'Hoole could fly so easily, but wreaked sheer havoc on an untrained owl.

And so it began. Soren and Martin swooped low, dodged a cresting wave, and scampered over another. The Barn Owl followed. She was better at this than they had expected. She was not as good as they were, but she was powerful, and she had been eating better than they had. She had more energy. Soren fleetingly wondered where Twilight was. But no, he had to fight this battle himself. Yet he could feel himself growing tired, and he could see that Martin was, too.

Then Soren had an idea. He would try to back her into the cliff just beneath them. The wind was dead there except for some odd pockets where the air was sucked suddenly downward into whirlpools. He knew where the pockets were, but she didn't. Perhaps he could dance her around and then back her right into one of these pockets. This was his last hope. Her battle claws were getting closer and closer each time she approached. Now she was coming in again full speed. He sheered off toward the cliffs and then dove. She followed. Somewhere he found a reserve of new strength. It flooded into his hollow bones. His gizzard tingled. *Follow me, follow me,* he thought.

It was working! She was confused, he could tell. Martin, always quick to pick up on things, began pressing in on her tail feathers. But just as they had led her to the edge of a pocket, a shadow slid across the cliffs. The fog dissolved and the moonlight blazed off a hard shiny surface. It was Kludd. His metal-sheathed face was almost blinding as the moon hit it. Blades of light sliced the night. It was impossible to see. Owl eyes were made for darkness, not this hot, gleaming light. Martin seemed to spin out of control. Another owl was at Kludd's side. Soren recognized him from the battle to rescue Ezylryb in the forest of Ambala. It was the one called Wortmore. But then, through the blinding light, something began to glow, a sinuous, glowing scroll of green.

"Slynella!" Soren screeched.

"Sssso pleased to be of help." The forked tongue of two colors split the night, and suddenly Wortmore folded his wings and dropped into the sea. His dark eyes turned crimson as an infinitesimally small drop of poison ravaged his body.

"Nyra, get out of here!" Kludd shrieked.

And then everything was quiet. Martin and Soren settled on an outcropping to catch their breath. "Oh, my goodness," Soren gasped. "Twice saved by poison!"

"You're a sight for sore eyes, Slynella." Martin's voice was quaking with relief. "How did you know to come?"

"Hortensssse. One of her dreamssss, you know."

Soren blinked. "Her dreams?"

"Yes, you know about Hortenssse and her dreamsss. She sssseees the truth sssssometimesss in her ssssleep. What she dreamsss often happensss."

And then Soren realized that what he dreamed had happened. The moon-faced owl in his dream that had appeared with Kludd was the same one that had appeared in his dream, first as a spider and then as the owl who spoke those frightening words, "A bit of your own medicine." Had his and Hortense's dreams somehow collided? Had they flown in their sleep into some shared dreamscape? Had their imaginations blended in this story of death and destruction?

But now he sensed that something was still not right. This owl who flew with Kludd had killed. He just knew it. She had come with a streak of blood across her face.

"It seems so quiet," Soren said.

"Is it over?" Martin wondered aloud. Was the siege finally over?

At that moment Gylfie and Twilight flew onto the ledges under the cliff.

"Is it over?" Martin asked again.

"We think so," Twilight replied. "But the Strix Struma Strikers suffered some heavy losses."

"Losses?" Martin said weakly.

"Not Ruby, not Otulissa?" Soren said.

"Not Ruby or Otulissa." Digger had just flown onto the ledge of the cliffs. "But Strix Struma has been killed."

CHAPTER TWENTY-FOUR

A New Constellation Rises

Otulissa's face was stony. Her white spots stood out like small hard pebbles.

"Do you think she's going to be all right, Soren?" Eglantine whispered. "You know how much she loved Strix Struma."

"I think so." He really wasn't sure, but he wanted to reassure his younger sister. He was worried. They were all worried about Otulissa. The young Spotted Owl had been flying beside her commander when Strix Struma was struck. It was talon-to-talon fighting, but within the first few blows, the enemy had ripped a tremendous gouge at the point where the primary feathers joined the body. Strix Struma's wing was almost severed and completely useless, but still she flew. Otulissa counterattacked bravely and managed to land a slashing blow across the attacker's face.

"I tried to save her," Otulissa told them when they visited her in her hollow. She kept repeating those words.

Digger, Twilight, Soren, and Gylfie didn't know what to

say. Then Mrs. Plithiver slithered in. "Otulissa, my dear, she did not want to be saved. What kind of a life would she have had with one wing? Could she have continued to lead the navigation chaw? Could she have commanded her brave Strix Struma Strikers? She had led a full life. She was old. She was ready. She died fighting for a great cause. Try not to fret, dear."

As comforting as the words had sounded to the other owls, Soren knew they had done nothing to relieve Otulissa's grief. And now as they gathered for the Final Ceremony, as the rites for a dead owl were called, he could see that Otulissa did not feel any better. Her utter stillness was unnerving. If he had not known better, he would have thought she had been carved in stone.

Meanwhile, a mere ten or twelve feet away on the balcony in the Great Hollow, Dewlap sobbed convulsively. "I never thought. I never thought," she kept sputtering. Now Otulissa moved. She swung her head around and puffed up in fury. "No, you never thought!" she hissed.

Then Barran flew to the highest perch. "We come to pay tribute today to a great Spotted Owl, Strix Struma. Although she and I were different species, we were sisters bound in our love of freedom and the pure joy of the pursuit of the knowledge of the stars that cycle endlessly, season upon season, in our night skies. It was from dear Strix

Struma, our navigation ryb, that I first learned about the "eyes of glaumora," as we often call the stars. It is the hideous fury of war that has brought her end, though one cannot call it an untimely death, for she had a long and a vigorous life." Barran continued to speak most lovingly about her long friendship with the Spotted Owl, and then it was Ezylryb's turn.

"Her Majesty Barran spoke of the hideous fury of war that brought down our beloved soldier Strix Struma. She died with her claws on. You have heard Barran refer to Strix Struma as her sister, and I am glad she did this. For we have just been fighting a war that was instigated by the vile notion that declares that some breeds of owls are better than others, are more pure. Not one of us shall ever again say the word 'pure' or 'purity' without thinking of the bloodshed these words have caused.

"We know that one breed or species of owl is not better or more pure than another. We are all of us sisters and brothers in owlkind. I mean to turn that word around and speak of the pureness of spirit of our dear friend, our fierce warrior Strix Struma, who died protecting those very values.

"Last night an owl perished, but on this night, a new constellation rises. Fly out now, young'uns, and find her in the stars that she so loved."

The night was crisp and clear as the owls flew out of the great hollow. Soren remembered his first navigation class with Strix Struma when they had traced the Golden Talons. Otulissa flew off by herself. Ruby, with whom she had grown so close during their time together in the Strikers, began to follow her.

"No, let her be, Ruby," Soren said, gliding up to her and touching her wing tip with his own.

"Come, young'uns!" Bubo suddenly appeared. "I hear there is a grand old forest fire blazing on the Broken Talon Point. Ezylryb says we should go have a look. Come along, Twilight, Digger, and the rest of you. We'll let you all fly with the colliering chaw tonight. Might learn a thing or two, eh?" He winked at Twilight.

They were halfway to the point when they caught sight of a young Spotted Owl. She was directly overhead.

"It's Otulissa!" Eglantine said.

"What is she doing out here? I didn't think she wanted to come," Soren said, flipping his head backward and straight up. Above was a group of stars he had never seen before. Thickly scattered, the stars spread out into two mirror image spirals — just like the smallest dots on a Spotted Owl's head.

"What is that?" Soren asked Bubo.

"Oh, maybe you have never flown this far north and east. There are different constellations here."

"What do they call it?" Soren asked.

"Oh, I forget right now. I think it's named after one of the snow flowers that grows up north at the edge of the glaciers. But I've never seen so many stars in it as tonight."

Some might have called it a flower, Soren thought. *But tonight it has changed forever.* He watched as Otulissa began to trace with the tip of one wing the spotted head that rose in the night.

Dawn had broken and a rosy pink flooded into the hollow. Soren stirred in his sleep. He had been dreaming terrible gizzard-shattering nightmares. The owl who held the moon in her face blinded him. It was like being moon blinked within his own dreams. He felt himself freeze and go yeep. He could not escape the dream.

A cold wind blew in through the hollow opening and brushed his face feathers. He blinked his eyes open. In an instant, he knew what he must do. Quietly, he rose and slipped out of the hollow and flew down to the entrance of Otulissa's hollow.

Otulissa was at her desk, writing. Her hollowmates were sound asleep. She looked up.

"It was the moon-faced owl who killed her wasn't it, Otulissa?"

She nodded. "They call her Nyra. She is your brother's mate."

"I know," Soren said.

Otulissa blinked. "How do you know?"

"I dreamed it."

"Then you have what they call the starsight," she said. "You dream about things and sometimes they happen. I've read about it. The stars, for you, are like little holes in the cloth of a dream."

Soren nodded. The way Otulissa had described it seemed right. "That blood across Nyra's face, you did that, Otulissa?"

"Yes, but it was just a little wound. Hardly mortal. Nyra attacked you after she killed Strix Struma, then she and your brother both got away." She paused. "They aren't finished with us, Soren. We can't wait for them."

"What do you mean?" A tremor passed through his gizzard.

"I mean that we can't fight defensively. We have to go after them."

Soren blinked. There was a fierceness in Otulissa's eyes. "What are you writing?"

"A plan — an invasion plan. I'm different now, Soren."
Her words came in a hot whisper. One of her hollowmates
stirred. "I've changed," she said softly, but her voice was
deadly. Soren turned to leave.

Otulissa called after him. "Dream, Soren, dream.
Dream your starsight dreams. Dream for your life, dream
for our lives. Dream for the Guardians of Ga'Hoole."

OWLS
and others
from

GUARDIANS *of* GA'HOOLE
The Siege

The Band

SOREN: Barn Owl, *Tyto alba,* from the Forest Kingdom of Tyto; escaped from St. Aegolius Academy for Orphaned Owls; training to be a Guardian at the Great Ga'Hoole Tree

GYLFIE: Elf Owl, *Micranthene whitneyi,* from the desert kingdom of Kuneer; escaped from St. Aegolius Academy for Orphaned Owls; Soren's best friend; training to be a Guardian at the Great Ga'Hoole Tree

TWILIGHT: Great Gray Owl, *Strix nebulosa,* free flier, orphaned within hours of hatching; training to be a Guardian at the Great Ga'Hoole Tree

DIGGER: Burrowing Owl, *Speotyto cunicularius*, from the desert kingdom of Kuneer; lost in desert after attack in which his brother was killed by owls from St. Aegolius; training to be a Guardian at the Great Ga'Hoole Tree

The Leaders of the Great Ga'Hoole Tree
BORON: Snowy Owl, *Nyctea scandiaca*, the King of Hoole

BARRAN: Snowy Owl, *Nyctea scandiaca*, the Queen of Hoole

EZYLRYB: Whiskered Screech Owl, *Otus trichopsis*, the wise weather-interpretation and colliering ryb (teacher) at the Great Ga'Hoole Tree; Soren's mentor (also known as LYZE OF KIEL)

STRIX STRUMA: Spotted Owl, *Strix occidentalis*, the dignified navigation ryb at the Great Ga'Hoole Tree

DEWLAP: Burrowing Owl, *Speotyto cunicularius*, the Ga'Hoolology ryb at the Great Ga'Hoole Tree

SYLVANA: Burrowing Owl, *Speotyto cunicularius*, a young ryb at the Great Ga'Hoole Tree

Others at the Great Ga'Hoole Tree

OTULISSA: Spotted Owl, *Strix occidentalis*, a student of prestigious lineage at the Great Ga'Hoole Tree

MARTIN: Northern Saw-whet Owl, *Aegolius acadicus*, in Ezylryb's chaw with Soren

RUBY: Short-eared Owl, *Asio flammeus*, in Ezylryb's chaw with Soren

EGLANTINE: Barn Owl, *Tyto alba*, Soren's younger sister

PRIMROSE: Pygmy Owl, *Glaucidium californicum*, Eglantine's best friend

MADAME PLONK: Snowy Owl, *Nyctea scandiaca*, the elegant singer of the Great Ga'Hoole Tree

BUBO: Great Horned Owl, *Bubo virginianus*, the blacksmith of the Great Ga'Hoole Tree

MRS. PLITHIVER: blind snake, formerly the nest-maid for Soren's family; now a member of the harp guild at the Great Ga'Hoole Tree

OCTAVIA: Kielian snake, nest-maid for Madame Plonk and Ezylryb

The Pure Ones

KLUDD: Barn Owl, *Tyto alba*, Soren's older brother; leader of the Pure Ones (also known as Metal Beak and High Tyto)

NYRA: Barn Owl, *Tyto alba*, Kludd's mate

WORTMORE: Barn Owl, *Tyto alba*, a Pure Guard lieutenant

Leaders of St. Aegolius Academy for Orphaned Owls

SKENCH: Great Horned Owl, *Bubo virginianus*, the Ablah General of St. Aegolius Academy for Orphaned Owls

SPOORN: Western Screech Owl, *Otus kennicottii*, first lieutenant to Skench

AUNT FINNY: Snowy Owl, *Nyctea scandiaca*, pit guardian at St. Aegolius

UNK: Great Horned Owl, *Bubo virginianus*, pit guardian at St. Aegolius

Others at the St. Aegolius Academy for Orphaned Owls

GRIMBLE: Boreal Owl, *Aegolius funerus*, captured as an adult by St. Aegolius patrols and held as a hostage with the promise that his family would be spared; killed when

Soren and Gylfie escaped from St. Aegolius Academy for Orphaned Owls

HORTENSE: Spotted Owl, *Strix occidentalis*, performed heroic acts at St. Aegolius (also known as Mist)

Other Characters

SIMON: Brown Fish Owl, *Ketupa (Bubo) zeylonensis*, a pilgrim owl of the Glauxian Brothers of the Northern Kingdoms

THE ROGUE SMITH OF SILVERVEIL: Snowy Owl, *Nyctea scandiaca*, a blacksmith not attached to any kingdom in the owl world

STREAK: Bald eagle, free flier

ZAN: Bald eagle and mate of Streak; mute

SLYNELLA: Flying snake whose venom is lifesaving when administered correctly

Look for

GUARDIANS *of* GA'HOOLE

BOOK FIVE

The Shattering

by Kathryn Lasky

Coming this August!

Is there a spy in the Great Ga'Hoole Tree?

In the ongoing deadly conflict between the evil Pure Ones and the brave owls of Ga'Hoole, the enemy seems to know Ga'Hoolian plans almost as they are made. Then, just as Soren begins to notice the strange behavior of his sister, Eglantine, and to suspect she is somehow in the power of the enemy, she disappears. Soren must lead the Chaw of Chaws to rescue her. Thus begins the next battle deep in the treacherous territory known as The Beaks, where a raging forest fire will prove to be the greatest threat to the rescuers — and their best hope for success.

About the Author

KATHRYN LASKY has had a long fascination with owls. Several years ago, she began doing extensive research about these birds and their behaviors — what they eat, how they fly, how they build or find their nests. She thought that she would someday write a nonfiction book about owls illustrated with photographs by her husband, Christopher Knight. She realized, though, that this would indeed be difficult since owls are nocturnal creatures, shy and hard to find. So she decided to write a fantasy about a world of owls. But even though it is an imaginary world in which owls can speak, think, and dream, she wanted to include as much of their natural history as she could.

Kathryn Lasky has written many books, both fiction and nonfiction. She has collaborated with her husband on such nonfiction books as *Sugaring Time,* for which she won a Newbery Honor; *The Most Beautiful Roof in the World;* and most recently, *Interrupted Journey: Saving Endangered Sea Turtles.* Among her fiction books are *The Night Journey,* a winner of the National Jewish Book Award; *Beyond the Burning Time,* an ALA Best Book for Young Adults; *True North: A*

Journey to the New World; Dreams in the Golden Country; and *Porkenstein.* She has written for the My Name Is America series, *The Journal of Augustus Pelletier: The Lewis and Clark Expedition, 1804,* and several books for The Royal Diary series including *Elizabeth I: Red Rose of the House of Tudor, England, 1544,* and *Jahanara, Princess of Princesses, India, 1627.* She has also received the *Boston Globe* Horn Book Award as well as the *Washington Post* Children's Book Guild Award for her contribution to nonfiction.

Lasky and her husband live in Cambridge, Massachusetts.

Out of the darkness a hero will rise.

Dragons and Deception!

A new series from Emily Rodda, author of *Deltora Quest* and *Deltora Shadowlands*!

DRAGONS OF DELTORA

Once the Dragons of Deltora ruled the land. Now only they can save it.

Dragons of Deltora #1: Dragon's Nest

In stores May 2004!

A Box. A Key. A Cryptic Note.

That's all twins Andrew and Evie received on their eleventh birthday, the day their mother vanished. Now the contents of the box will lead them on an incredible journey in the search for their mom — and into a world where no one's identity can be trusted.

Spy X #1: The Code

In stores June 2004!

SCHOLASTIC

DD/SXT

Other Series Worth Screaming About...

Garth Nix
The KEYS to the KingDom

The key to a house no one can see — and a mystery that must be solved.

Emily Rodda
DELTORA QUEST

A land of magic — and monsters.

Emily Rodda
DELTORA SHADOWLANDS

An epic fight against forces of darkness.

K.A. Applegate
REMNANTS™

The end of the world has come...and gone.

SCHOLASTIC

FANTT